THE LYN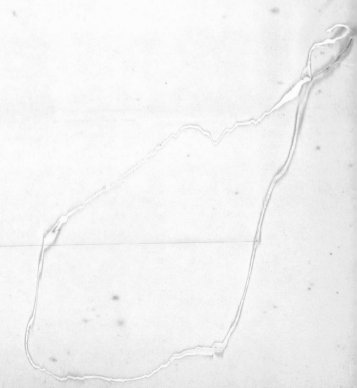

T. P. O'MAHONY

The Lynch Years

A Political Fantasy

THE DOLMEN PRESS

Set in Palatino type by Redsetter Limited, Dublin
and printed by Billing & Sons Ltd.
for the publishers,

The Dolmen Press Limited
Mountrath, Portlaoise, Ireland

Designed by Liam Miller

First published 1986

ISBN 0 85105 449 8

The Dolmen Press receives financial assistance from
The Arts Council, An Comhairle Ealaíon, Ireland

To the class of 1953 at Blackpool NS —
quintessential Lynch territory

INTRODUCTION

The unpublished memoirs of Dr Ernst Lubbocks – on which this novel is based – came into my possession in the early part of 1985 during a visit to East Berlin. In a pub just off Alexanderplatz they were handed to me by a young blonde stripper whose act I had watched and applauded the previous night. As she autographed the club programme for me (striptease acts are forbidden in East Germany and so have become clandestine and part of the 'black economy') she asked me where I came from and what I did for a living. I told her I was Irish and a writer. She said she had something to give me. We made an assignation for the following day in a nearby pub. Thus it was that Dr Lubbocks' notebooks came my way.

All the young stripper would say by way of explanation was that Dr Lubbocks was a time-traveller, a man able to move easily through the years and the centuries. I had of course heard such people existed, but I had never had direct experience of them. One of their great gifts is to be able to discern and pass back and forth between parallel or 'alternative' versions of history.

It became evident after a quick perusal of the notebooks that Dr Lubbocks had concerned himself with Irish history – and several versions of it – from 1916 to the present time, with particular emphasis on the years from 1966 onwards.

Being something of a metaphysician, he has imposed his own cognitive structure on the events experienced by him with the result that he has achieved a cross-cutting effect between several parallel and, so far as I am concerned, equally valid accounts of what constitutes 'modern Ireland' – a creation of the imagination as much as anything else.

7

The narrative which follows is fiction insofar as I have taken liberties of interpretation, organisation, extrapolation and speculation with Dr Lubbocks' memoirs. The selection and method of presentation – and therefore the bias – is mine.

By the way, when I enquired of the stripper if her stage name – Lilli von Ossen – was real, she replied: 'No – my real name is Kathleen Houlihan'.

T. P. O'Mahony
Cork, Ireland
May 1986

PS: My thanks are due to the librarians of *The Irish Press*, *The Irish Times* and *The Boston Globe* for their assistance during research for this novel. And I must also express my gratitude to Vincent Browne for making material from *Magill* available to me and to Eamonn McCann of *The Sunday World* for a similar kindness.

"History may not be fiction, but that does not mean
that it is not a work of imagination."

William Irwin Thompson: *The Imagination of an Insurrection:
Dublin, Easter 1916.*

1

Meryl McClone is standing in pink bra and panties in front of a mirror in a bedroom in the Chelsea Hotel on East 17th Street in Manhattan when the news of Jack Lynch's resignation breaks.

It is 3.37 pm on December 7, 1979.

A tall, copper-haired, finely structured woman of 36, Ms McClone has just kissed her current lover – a radical playwright from Brooklyn – goodbye after a mid-afternoon tryst, and she is in the process of dressing herself when the ABC network news carries the Lynch item. Meryl had met him twice, in Dublin in 1970 and in New York when he addressed the United Nations in 1979. And, in the manner of many women, she had grown instantly fond of him.

'A sweet man,' she had called him at the time.

She remembers well his handshake and the way he held his pipe when he talked to her. And the soft gentle voice. She knows some people think Lynch is a pushover, but they are wrong about that. Dead wrong.

'Fuck!'

She remembers her project.

Lynch's resignation as Taoiseach will mean a change of approach. She looks at her watch and picks up the red stilettos from under the bed.

It is time to call San Francisco.

She steps into the high-heels.

'I want to make a person-to-person call,' she tells the operator. 'The other party is Gene Finkleheim and the number is . . . .'

While she waits she cradles the telephone against her face and reaches across for the pack of Virginia

Slims in her handbag.

A lighter flares.

Looking at her reflection in the mirror, Ms McClone thinks she has put on weight. Her boobs in particular seem bigger these days. Perhaps it is the Pill. Either way, Alfonso Seagull, her lover, is keen as hell on her tits.

She has her hand on the left one when San Francisco replies.

It is Gene.

'Hi . . . yeah, I know . . . I take it you've already heard out there on the West Coast about Jck Lynch? . . . No! . . . well, he's resigned . . . yeah, he's gone . . . I don't know where it leaves us . . . I'll have to talk to the studio . . . can we meet more or less immediately if necessary . . . ?'

Finkleheim, who is still in bed after a very late night, says he will call her back later.

She turns away to look for her jeans and sweater, an expression of faint puzzlement on her face. She and Finkleheim have worked together on the Northern Ireland 'troubles' on and off since 1970 – the year of the sensational Arms Trial in Dublin, a trial not unconnected with the growth of the Provisional IRA and a new phase in the armed struggle for a United Ireland.

At that time they worked for Canadian television. Later they formed a freelance partnership – reflecting the intimate state of their own personal relationship – and then later on joined the ABC network.

That was in 1977, the year Jack Lynch brought Fianna Fáil ('Soldiers of Destiny') back into power in the Irish Republic with a 20-seat majority in a Parliament of 148 seats, the biggest majority of any leader in the history of the State.

FLASHBACK: The bar of Buswell's Hotel in Molesworth Street, directly across from Leinster House where Dáil Éireann sits, is crowded. New Dáil Deputies with their wives and girlfriends are milling about. The air is heavy with the relief, joy and arrogance of victory, and replete with grandiloquent talk of new beginnings and new times ahead. The time is 4.13 pm. It is Friday, June 9, 1977, the day after the Election Count. And there is no mistaking the outcome. The National Coalition Government headed by Liam Cosgrave, which has ruled the Republic since 1973, is devastated. And the man of the moment is Jack Lynch.

Among the crowd in Buswell's are several dozen journalists including Meryl McClone and Gene Finkleheim. As they wait to interview Lynch they drink Guinness and talk of their plans for a major documentary for American television on the Irish situation. The working title which they have chosen for the project is 'Where The Shamrock Dare Not Grow'. This will be changed in due course by an editor at ABC, a graduate of Yale University who is totally ignorant of Irish affairs, to 'The Shamrock Soldiers'. The change will bring a threat of resignation from McClone and Finkleheim, but to no avail. American TV is like that; nobody gives a shit and there are no principles anymore.

If you wish you may purchase a video tape of 'The Shamrock Soldiers' from ABC Video Sales in New York. The title stinks, but it's a damn good documentary.

Jack Lynch himself has said so.

2

In a third floor apartment on Telegraph Hill in the centre of San Francisco Gene Finkleheim is awakened by the buzzing of the computerized alarm at his bedside. He reaches out a hand in the darkness, gropes for the control and switches it off. The alarm is pre-set for 4.45 pm. It is now just over four hours since the call from Meryl McClone in New York.

Finkleheim's head hurts.

Last night he was out on the town and is now feeling a little sorry for himself. It's not just the drink; it's that bitch Janine, a divorcee he's been seeing who is complicating his life. For one thing, she refuses to go to bed with him. That's bad enough, but she keeps talking about marriage as well. Hell, she's already dumped two husbands, and her alimony payments are so good she can afford to buy 600 dollar leather trousers. The trouble is she keeps them on all the time . . . .

Finkleheim half rolls out of bed and switches on the overhead light.

He took her to Las Vegas once and she left him languishing for three days in a motel. He never found out what happened. She's like that, mysterious and unpredictable. Sinatra was in town singing at Caesar's Palace and Finkleheim speculates from time to time that Janine joined all the other groupies hanging around the hotel. It would be totally out of character for her, of course, but you can never tell with women like that.

Finkleheim's real trouble is that he's half in love with Janine and can't get her out of his system. If only he could lay her. At the same time he cannot abide the

14

thought of marriage.

Now here's another complication: Meryl McClone and the Jack Lynch project.

Finkleheim pulls himself out of bed and walks semi-naked (he's wearing his pyjama bottoms) to the friedge. He pours a large glass of orange juice and runs a hand through his black bushy hair. He's tall, thin and pale-faced with a tight beard that's showing patches of grey on both sides of his chin. On a bedside table he recovers his wire-rimmed spectacles and puts them on. Without them he can't see much. Both his eyes are weak, especially the right one. When he's drunk and morose – which is fairly often – he's inclined to worry about his sight, fearing that one of these days he'll go blind.

Janine laughs when he tells her this, mocking his fears. It was different when he lived with Meryl McClone. She understood him, most of the time anyway.

As he sips his orange juice and absent-mindedly glances at a copy of *Newsweek* on the bedroom floor he feels nostalgia for the days with Meryl. It should never have ended, he shouldn't have allowed it to. He blames himself.

At least we have the project, he tells himself, knowing that he is looking forward to seeing her again.

He'd have to tell Janine of course. She'd bitch a bit about his being away but it wouldn't really bother her. He was never sure if he was special to her. She had other men. Still, he hopes he'll be missed.

Before going back to sleep he had 'phoned Meryl back.

They arrange to meet in Boston in the Park Plaza Hotel. It is his idea. He doesn't explain over the 'phone, just says it is important. Meryl says okay.

15

He will wait until they meet in Boston before telling her of the Teddy Kennedy document. Or perhaps it should be called 'The Chappaquiddick Document'.

If it exists.

It has to.

It is the only explanation.

Finkleheim is worrying again, but it is too early in the morning and his head still hurts.

He searches for the coffee jar and reminds himself to ring Janine and tell her he's going to be out of town for a while.

From the front cover of *Newsweek* Sissy Spacek winks at him.

3

The script is only half-written. In fact, it's little more than a bundle of notes. Not that Alfonso Seagull is bothered. He likes the creative process, taking half-formed concepts and turning them into dramatic constructs, and doing it piecemeal, feeding off the others in his circle, bouncing ideas back and forth and setting up a chemistry of what he calls 'dramaturgical tension'. They're his words, not mine.

He strides purposefully across the stage to where Alana is sitting.

A small man going prematurely bald, he has a round smooth face with small piercing black eyes. Almost all the time he wears denim clothes and canvas running shoes.

Alana takes one of the cigarettes from the box he holds out. They're an Egyptian brand, long and pale brown. As she lights it Seagull turns away, intense and preoccupied.

She draws deeply on the cigarette and waits patiently, smoke filtering through her nostrils. She's 41 and big-boned, her short hair tinted bright purple. She is not only Seagull's favourite actress, she is also a woman whose judgement he trusts and whose collaboration he seeks. She enjoys a formidable reputation in off-off-Broadway theatrical circles, though hers doesn't quite match Seagull's.

Somewhere in her background there is Irish blood – her surname is actually Cahill though she uses Leone as a stage name, a kind of tribute to the director of "The Good, The Bad and The Ugly" which she loves.

It is the presence of Irish blood which excites Seagull. He is himself of German-Italian extraction, but Ireland and the Irish hold a special and abiding interest for him. He can offer no rational explanation for this. Yet it is undoubtedly one of the reasons – perhaps the main reason – why he is fascinated almost to the point of obsession by Meryl McClone, a woman who was actually born in County Donegal out near Gweedore.

When she was only three her family emigrated to the USA, settling first in Illinois and then moving to New York State. Seagull met her for the first time in Manhattan at a publisher's party on Lexington Avenue. He got her number from someone at the party and rang her the next day for a date.

A week later she revealed her magnificent tits to him for the first time and his world went topsy-turvy.

To date his ardour has shown no sign of cooling.

'Art must be accusation, expression, passion,' declares Seagull from the back of the stage. He waves the sheaf of papers in his hand.

Alana watches in silence. She knows there will be hours of this, hours when he is tormented by the need to create, and hours when he will be unbearable.

She knows it's different when Meryl McClone, the copper-haired Irish beauty, is around. And she longs for her presence mainly because it serves as a carthasis for Seagull. McClone's effect on him has a way of releasing pent-up energies. Alana has witnessed this herself. She knows the gorgeous Irish woman is good for Seagull. She also knows she herself could be good for Meryl McClone. If only she had the chance.

'Without accusation, without bringing a hard cutting edge to bear on history, tearing it to shreds and re-fashioning it, irrespective of the cost to presuppositions or the implications for our sacred cows, art is nothing. Just shit . . . dung . . . excrement . . . .'

Seagull is addressing rows of empty seats.

'We artists are called on to refashion everything, especially history. It is our sacred task to rewrite history from the inside out, to burst through all the conventions like a cock through a virgin's hymen. History cries out to be deflowered!'

Alana draws on her cigarette. The beat of her heart has increased. She remains outwardly calm, showing no emotion.

Alfonso Seagull draws near.

They are alone in the Jan Hus Theatre on East 74th Street in Manhattan.

Seagull goes on his knees in front of Alana. The overhead lights exaggerate the sheen of perspiration on his face. His eyes are bright, focused, glaring.

'Marry me, beloved, and we will away to some green isle where I will to the end of time write dirty poems for you in between fucking you seventeen times a day Sundays included . . . .'

'Piss off, Alfonso.'

'Must you always reject me so?'

18

'Get off your knees, you fool.'

'Woman, you are hard-hearted,' says Seagull, rising.

'Where do we go from here?'

'We could go boating on the East River – have you ever lost your knickers in a boat?'

'Don't be daft.'

'It's just my magnanimous nature.'

'Are we doing this for television or the stage?' asks Alana, holding up the half-completed script.

'For the theatre of course,' replies Seagull, all business again. 'Miss McClone is doing something for television. What I want to do is a play about two journalists who are working on something to do with Ireland for television.'

Alana consults the script.

'Who is Jack Lynch?'

Seagull's hand flies to his head in a gesture of utter astonishment.

'Dear lady, your knowledge of matters pertaining to the theatre and indeed to the cinema is profound, almost mind-boggling, but you are sorely lacking in awareness of the wider world, dare I say the real world, at least as reality is conventionally perceived . . . '

'I'm still asking – who is Jack Lynch?'

'Oh holy fuck!'

Alana is unperturbed. This time she lights one of her own cigarettes, a Marlboro.

Seagull does an about-turn and paces very deliberately across the stage, away from Miss Cahill-Leone.

'Jack Lynch is an alien being from some far-off galaxy who landed in a flying saucer – it was the same colour as your hair – in a field outside the village of Timoleague in the County of Cork which is the biggest and brightest and the best County in the glorious Republic of Ireland – colour it pea-green.'

'How very interesting,' remarks Alana drily.

'I kid you not. This man – for he chose the male form – confounded his enemies, bedazzled the Irish people with his genius, put a stop to cross-border pig smuggling, redesigned the shape of the Paddy whiskey bottle, and led the great Irish nation to several all-night parties in Croke Park. In his spare time he also auctioned off the flying saucer to the Russians and with the proceeds he built a monument to himself which to this day is known as Shandon Steeple. It stands up very straight and they say it's full of black pepper . . . .'

Alana blew three perfect smoke rings.

'They don't exist.'

'Who don't exist?'

'Aliens.'

'Are you sure?'

Seagull rushes across the stage and drops to his knees in front of Alana. 'Are you sure, dear lady? Are you absolutely sure, I mean rock-solid certain?'

'They don't exist,' she repeats, giving him a poker-faced look.

4

Dr Ernst Lubbocks would not have agreed with Miss Cahill-Leone. Indeed, he is in a position to prove her wrong, but that will have to wait.

Right now he has other things on his mind.

He is sitting at his desk aboard *Zintanza* high over the United States, a large map unfurled in front of him. Close at hand is a calculator and a large magnifying glass. And a cup of tea.

The Doctor sips the tea.

After a moment he shakes his head. He has been listening to the on-stage exchanges between Alana Leone and Alfonso Seagull.

'When will people learn?' he murmurs, half to himself.

The powerful, indeed magical, equipment on board the extraterrestrial spaceship of which he is owner, designer and captain has enabled him to eavesdrop on Seagull and the actress. This is the second day of the operation and Seagull has been deliberately chosen. Along with two others.

Even now Seagull's face is visible on one of the screens on the console in front of the Doctor. He switches the sound off. There will be plenty of talk later on.

On a yellow legal notepad the Doctor has jotted down some notes.

'December 7, 1979 – Jack Lynch resigns in Dublin . . . .'

He has added three other names:

'Meryl McClone (A).'

'Glen Finkleheim (B).'

'Alfonso Seagull (C).'

The Doctor turns to the tall woman standing just behind his left shoulder. 'Get me a fix on subjects A and B . . . .'

Ludmilla Erebus adjusts some of the controls on the main console. She is 25, blonde, and wears a tight-fitting black catsuit and black patent leather laced boots.

Images flicker across several of the screens.

The face of Meryl McClone appears. She looks tired. Now she smiles. Somebody is talking to her.

'Location?' asks the Doctor.

Ludmilla Erebus checks her instruments. 'New York City. Mid-Manhattan.'

'And the other?'

Another screen comes to life. It is filled with other images. Glen Finkleheim is recognisable. He is in a car driving away from the centre of San Francisco.

'Subject B is on the way to the airport in Frisco. We have established that he is booked on a flight to Boston,' intones Ludmilla.

The Doctor smiles and nods.

'All is going according to plan. Get me some more tea and ask my coordinator to join me.'

Ludmilla Erebus leaves the compartment. Doctor Lubbocks reaches forward and presses a switch. A third screen flickers into life and is again filled with the features of Alfonso Seagull. On the three screens in front of him Doctor Lubbocks is now watching Subjects A, B and C.

The miracles of modern technology never cease to please him, even when they are his own miracles.

Another blonde, even taller than Ludmilla, enters the compartment. Her hair is cut very short except for a central ridge which stands out from her head in spikes. She is dressed just like the other girl and looks younger, being in fact just 22. This is B. B. Bachinski Some – who are supposed to know about these things – say she is his daughter; others claim she is his lover. What is beyond dispute is that she is extremely beautiful.

She is carrying a large folder in her hand. The cover is blue and on it in large black capital letters are the words: THE LYNCH YEARS.

5

The Lubbocks' Diaries – Extract One:

The trouble with history is that it traps people, it inhibits and imprisons them. Which is why I have decided to intervene. I am a nice fellow really, but before we get to the end of this story I'll have to face some tough decisions. I'll have to sort some people out. Don't misunderstand. I'm not omnipotent. And – more's the pity - I can't change human nature. People are people. It's a truism but we're stuck with it. One of your intellectuals (you don't have very many) – I think it was Conor Cruise O'Brien – once said: "We are stuck with one another and with our various versions of our history." And that's true. That's the trouble.

You can regard me, if you like, as a sort of cosmic puppeteer, but I don't control all the strings. I have powers that go beyond your comprehension, but I don't have absolute power. That belongs to Another. And right now we're not talking. So I have to make do with what I've got. My intention? Well, if I'm motivated by anything it is by a desire to free people from the tyranny of the past. That's why I've chosen Jack Lynch and his time. He tried to do that too, in his own way. Oh I know you can argue all day and all night about how well he succeeded – or whether he succeeded at all. All I'm saying at this stage is that he tried, and is still trying. So let's be prepared to give him some bit of credit. If you feel differently at the end of this story, so be it.

Did you notice the folder at the end of the last scene, the one entitled "The Lynch Years"? That's our story, but it's your story too. Which is why I want to help. And why you must participate. To do that you have to put aside your preconceptions. I know that's not easy, of course not. But it's the only path forward. Believe me, I know what I'm talking about. We have to live out, through and beyond "The Lynch Years". All of us. More later.

6

Meryl McClone checks into the Park Plaza Hotel in Boston at 2.30 pm local time. The flight from La Guardia to Logan Airport was on schedule. On the way she slept for a while.

The desk clerk looks up from his ledger. No messages he tells her, in answer to her query. She isn't expecting any.

She wanders into the bar off the foyer. She's not hungry but decides a Bloody Mary will help. It's December and there's snow on the streets outside.

At the bar she asks for cigarettes but they don't have Virginia Slims. The bartender tells her there is a store close by. She sips the Bloody Mary and looks around. The bar is doing poor business.

Gene Finkleheim is due in from San Francisco in the evening. His room is already booked. The last time they stayed at a hotel together they shared a room. Not this time. Their lives have changed. Work is the dominant dimension, not romance. All the same, the memories linger.

She wonders if he has changed much. It's months since they met. These days the telephone is their only link, that and the pages of data and ideas for their project which they send back and forth to each other. She won't admit it, but she feels a sense of loss. Gene Finkleheim was – is – a good man, she thinks.

So is Alfonso Seagull, even though he is sexually

insatiable.

The thought of that makes her smile.

Last night he came around with his tape recorder and spent nearly two hours quizzing her about the documentary she and Gene are working on. Over and over he asked her the same question: 'Tell me what kind of guy Jack Lynch is – what makes him tick?'

She did her best to delineate his character and to list his strong and weak features.

Alfonso was satisfied at last and put the tape recorder away. 'Essential research for my new play,' he told her. 'I'm going to call it "The Green Ayatollah".'

'Not a bad title,' she tells him, though at this stage she has no idea what he is actually doing and she presumes the title isn't meant to refer to Lynch.

Before he left he made love to her on the living-room floor. Fortunately, it has a carpet. He came – as always. This time she couldn't.

All tension, she told herself.

She just told him she was off-colour.

He is no *outré*.

In mainstream theatre circles he is frowned on. Not everywhere. *The Village Voice* reviewed two of his plays and did a mini-profile of him. They said he was 'an angry iconoclast'.

How right they are. He's even angry when he makes love, she tells herself, smiling secretly.

She wonders what he will make of Irish history, or of what he will make of what they will make of Irish history.

That must wait.

Her thoughts turn again to Gene Finkleheim. The sense of anticipation grows. She is puzzled as to why he insisted that they meet in Boston.

There is just a little of the Bloody Mary left. She drains the glass. It is time to go and look for cigarettes.

She's glad of the heavy brown sheepskin coat she has with her. She buttons it up and leaves the hotel.

A watery sun is shining. The streets are a mess, covered in snow and slush.

Meryl picks her way gingerly along the sidewalk. A neon sign advertising Schlitz beer flashes in the distance. She heads for it. Perhaps there is a store close by. Just now though a bar is more attractive. She feels she needs diversion.

Inside it is dark and warm and cosy.

Meryl orders another Bloody Mary and is grateful for the pack of Virginia Slims.

Towards the back of the bar somebody is playing pool. Halfway along the counter a television set is on.

At 3 o'clock there is a newscast. The barman turns the sound up. It is mostly stuff about the Middle East.

When it comes to the national headlines there is another UFO story. These days they are commonplace.

Yet something about this one seems different, perhaps even credible.

According to the newescaster the UFO – described as a 'spaceship' – was spotted low down in the sky over a small town in Missouri, just outside St Louis.

The TV team even has an interview with an eye-witness, a young woman from the town. Her name is Linda Scott.

Asked what the spacecraft looks like, she replies 'It looked like, well, to tell the truth, it looked like a flying vibrator . . . .'

7

Meryl pulls back the plastic curtain and steps out.

She is naked.

In front of the full-length mirror she stands and admires her body, her hand resting on the tuft of reddish-brown hair between her thighs.

The hotel room is air-conditioned and the shower has refreshed her. Outside it is dark and cold and the cars around Boston Common have their headlights on. In a little over an hour Gene Finkleheim should be disembarking at Logan.

Meryl spent the afternoon along Boylston Street, visiting boutiques and bookshops after her sojourn in the bar. She has picked up a new biography of Maria Callas now lying open on a chair outside the shower.

The Callas-Onassis affair has touched chords in her own subconscious: her hands are now on her breasts, gently squeezing them, the nipples still erect from the water.

FLASHBACK: It is a lazy September afternoon in Louisiana, a warm muggy afternoon with the heat shimmering over the bayous and the silence punctuated by the bark of bull-frogs and the crackle of crickets. The lovers have escaped to the open country, leaving the politicians to the noise and razzmatazz of the Convention Hall in downtown New Orleans, the vast Superdrome where President Nixon is scheduled to speak in a matter of hours.

As Gene Finkleheim unclips Meryl McClone's black bra he has no thought at all for presidential matters or concerns. A single thought has taken possession of him. He is going to make love for the very first time to this wild, vibrant and lovely Irish girl whose charms have held him captive for months past.

Her superb breasts, all pale pinkness and dark brown nipples, spill out and he bends to apply his lips to them. His desire is nigh uncontrollable and he quivers with sexual tension.

As Meryl lifts her dress he manages after three attempts to unbuckle his belt and drop his trousers.

They are lying on a grassy hillock a mile from Interstate Highway 101 on the outskirts of New Orleans.

'Why did we have to come here?' gasps Gene as his unsteady hand guides his penis into Meryl's wet pussy. It's a question he doesn't really want an answer to.

Her strong thighs encircle him, pulling him deeper into her.

'I can't talk,' she tells him through clenched teeth, feeling his surging cock going right through her.

Any second now there will be a dual erotic explosion as they heave in unison on the grassy knoll, observed only by a disinterested jackdaw.

A 'phone rings.

Meryl, naked, momentarily flounders.

She picks up the instrument, the image of Gene's cock rapidly receding.

'Hello,' she says huskily, being slightly out of breath.

It is Lucette, her sister, calling from Cincinnatti.

'What's with you?'

'Did you hear on television about that spaceship?' asks Lucette, all excited. 'Isn't it weird?'

'I dunno,' replies Meryl, part of her mind still far away. 'We have these reports all the time now . . . .'

'I think this one's different.'

'Why, for godsakes?'

'I just have a feeling . . . .'

28

'Are you going through that psychic phase again?'

'Come on, sis, that's not fair.'

'Okay. So I'm sorry. Now what's the problem?'

Lucette is 20 and fanciful, whimsical and a worrier.

'Nothing. I just wanted to say hallo to you. And to talk about this spaceship. There's something really strange going on on board. I just know it. Something really far out!'

'You've been reading Ursula Le Guin again, haven't you?'

'And you have no romance in your soul,' retorts Lucette, an avid reader of science fiction.

'I don't know about that,' muses Meryl, thinking of Gene Finkleheim again and a special part of his anatomy. 'You could be wrong there . . . anyway, tell me about life in downtown Cincinnatti . . . how are all the men in your life . . . .?'

8

'I have this idea, see. You take two terrorists, two women, smart and sexy, and you dress them up as nuns. First, though, you've got to have a plan. Remember Dealey Plaza in Dallas and the assassination of President Kennedy in 1963? Now there's plans for you. All that shit about Lee Harvey Oswald was just a put-up job. So we need a blueprint – a blueprint for assassination. That's going to be the background to the play.'

Alfonso Seagull smiles in a self-satisfied way and looks at Alana who has kicked off one of her high heels and is scratching her foot.

'So what's the plan?' she asks, straightening up.

'I'm still tossing it around, so bear with me. But I figure the UN building is the best place to knock off Lynch. You remember Hitchcock used it in "North by Northwest"?'

'One of my favourites,' says Alana. 'I love Cary Grant.'

'Okay. So we locate Lynch there. What was that date? You know, the time he came to New York to address the UN?'

Alana goes through the sheaf of notes on her lap. 'I have it here somewhere . . . here it is . . . it was November 1979.'

'Great. That was a good year. We all had a collective orgasm because of the Pope. Are you a Catholic? Jesus, in all this time I've never once asked you. How many times have we humped? Never mind, that's a complicated sub-plot . . . .'

Alana giggles. They've stopped going to bed now, but there was a time . . . .

As a matter of fact I am a Catholic, she reminds herself.

Seagull is back on the rails. 'We'll open with the terrorists planning the hit in Dublin. Or maybe Belfast. The backroom of a pub somewhere. Plenty of stuff on Lynch. Loads of colourful revolutionary rhetoric, especially from the one woman present. She's gonna be "The Green Ayatollah", though every-body will be looking for a man. That's gonna be one of the surprises . . . .'

'Will that work?' asks Alana who is busy taking notes.

'Sure. Why the hell not? She could be a cross between Jane Fonda and whoever is the top Provo broad at the moment. Good-looking but tough and able and very, very determined. And all of that comes out of anger and frustration. She must be a real hard

30

lady, cold and ruthless, the kind of woman who would have no fucking qualms about planting a bomb in the middle of Macys or Bloomingdales on Christmas Eve . . . .'

'A kind of Patty Hearst in green . . . .?'

'Hearst was an amateur compared to some of these women in Belfast. And it's always been like that in Ireland – tough broads in the movement for freedom down through the years . . . .'

'I wonder what they were like in bed?'

'Jesus Christ, Alana . . . !'

'I mean it. You know this theory that Joan Baez has about love-making and war-making . . . .?'

'Fuck Joan Baez.'

'If that's how you feel . . . .'

'Concentrate woman, control that libido of yours. Did you know that during the Treaty debates in Dáil Éireann in 1921-22 the most unrelenting, the most uncompromising speeches came from women? Oh yeah, those women were like iron and just as black. Man, they were implacable. They could make De Valera look like a softie. Imagine that. Think about it because that's the kind of woman we must create.'

'It could be a great part, maybe even a Tony-winning part.'

'Right. Who knows? The big thing, though, is to build in a lot of tension, and the way to do that is to set up a dialectic, to have very strong arguments against killing Lynch. That stuff will write itself. The central strand of the dialectic will be the view that to assassinate Lynch would be hugely counter-productive and instead of destablizing the Republic would have the contrary effect. It would lead to a massive clampdown on subversives, the introduction of internment without trial in the South, and maybe even a mandatory death sentence for certain categories of killings . . . .'

31

'It sounds like a tract for 1798, or passages from the Warren Commission Report.'

'Maybe we could incorporate some of that stuff, rewrite it or whatever, or at least draw parallels with Dallas using old newsreel footage as a backdrop.'

'What about the two nuns?'

'That's where we switch to New York. A lot will have happened during the interim. And by this stage we're setting the stage for the assassination. Enter the two nuns; they're the hit squad.'

'I have a great idea.'

'Shoot.'

'We could have them register at some Eastside hotel using the names Jacqueline Kennedy and Marina Oswald.'

'Wouldn't that be a dead giveaway?'

'Why? Ghoulish, maybe. But what's wrong with ghoulish?'

'Don't you think a couple of professionals would go in the other direction and pick names like Mary Brown or Anne Jones or something as ordinary as that . . . .?'

'I'm not sure it works like that. And it's only a play anyway. It's not like it's for real . . . .'

'Yeah, it's only a play. But what is fucking real?'

9

The Lubbocks' Diaries – Extract Two:
That girl has class. Lucette, I mean. The girl in Cincinnatti. If we had a few more like her around we could get this tired old clapped-out planet moving again. There used to be women like that in Ireland once, fair-haired maidens

who were children of the old religion and who understood the Seventh Dimension and the ways of the old gods. The Celtic gods. That's all gone now, or going. If you talk about banshees or succubi people just think you're mad and start sending for the men in the white coats.

Lucette is wired into all of that, she's switched on. The others just live impoverished lives, chasing the all-powerful dollar or something called success. I like that girl. I must keep an eye on her. Where I come from she'd be big time. She possesses what the alchemists call 'prescience'. Mark my words.

10

Gene Finkleheim, tieless, rosy-cheeked from the cold, and with his black overcoat flapping about him, hurries in. He's carrying a red 'Oakland Raiders' canvas hold-all and a slim leather and chrome brief-case.

As he comes into the relative warmth of the bar of the Park Plaza Hotel his spectacles start to mist up. He drops his gear, whips them off and searches for a handkerchief.

Where the hell is Meryl?

The specs go back on again. Outside it's snowing gently.

He spots her at the far end of the counter. She's looking straight at him, her hand held up.

He picks up his gear and hurries down to her. She knows he's excited; it's all over his face. She tries to think of an old Mae West line, just to stop him in his tracks, but it won't come so she abandons the idea. He's as untidy and as unkempt as ever, she tells herself as he approaches. For all that, she's very glad to see him.

'Hallo Gene,' she murmurs.

Awkwardly he kisses her on the mouth.

'Hello Meryl. You're looking great. Super.'

'I feel fine. How are you?'

'Rushing around as always,' he grins.

Meryl likes his grins: they make him look like a schoolboy.

'So tell me.'

She tries, badly, to hide her impatience.

'Let me get a drink first. How about you?'

'I'll have another Bloody Mary.'

'Still on that stuff – huh?'

'That's me.'

He summons the bartender and orders Meryl's drink and a Jack Daniels for himself with a beer chaser.

'Why all the mystery on the 'phone?'

'Let's go over here,' he tells her, indicating a table.

They cross over to the table and he whips off his overcoat. Picking up the briefcase, he unclasps it and extracts a folder. Meryl lights a cigarette.

'How was the flight?' she asks, as she waits for him to sort himself out.

'Fine,' he murmurs, 'just fine.'

The folder is open. Photostats are revealed.

Gene Finkleheim gathers himself. 'Do you remember the last time I came up here to Boston to do some research?'

Meryl exhales smoke and nods. 'Sure I do.' They had talked on the 'phone about it. A newspaper colleague from Boston had rung Gene; he knew they were doing a project on Ireland. He said there was a woman in Boston Gene should talk to – a policeman's widow. Mrs Mary Cooney. She now worked as a

34

cleaning lady at Boston College, the Jesuit-run institution.

'I never told you what happened,' explains Gene, 'because at the time it was all a bit untidy, with loose ends all over the place, and I didn't really know what to make of it . . . .'

He pauses to sip some whiskey. 'Anyway, here's what happened. I made an appointment with Mrs Cooney at the College and took a taxi over there. Now at this stage I didn't know what I was looking for or what it was that she was supposed to know. My pal here in Boston who put me on to her didn't know either, or if he did he wasn't telling me. To tell the truth, I don't think he knew. Otherwise he wouldn't have shared the information with me. He'd have gone and done the story for his own paper.'

'There is a story then?'

'A damn good one – if we can corroborate it. And that's not going to be easy.'

Meryl gave him her full attention now; she could sense his intensity.

'The background is this. It seems Mrs Cooney's husband dies in what are called "suspicious circumstances" back in 1969 just after Chappaquiddick.'

'Chappaquiddick? What's that got to do with it?

'Everything. Or nothing. Depends on what we can come up with. Here's what happened, though I'm filling in some of the blank spaces as I go along. When Teddy Kennedy went off the bridge at Chappaquiddick with Mary Jo Kopechne in July 1969 a briefcase – or some documents from same – went missing from the car. Okay?'

Meryl nods. The unexpected introduction of the Kennedy name has sent a *frisson* through her. She senses that this could be big stuff.

35

'Four days later Cooney is killed in the centre of Boston. He gets himself run down on Beacon Street. A hit and run. Why? After all, it could just be an accident. They happen all the time. There was nothing much in Cooney's background to suggest he might be a target for a hitman or have a contract out on him. He was a run-of-the-mill Irish-American cop, not into any heavy stuff. It is true that he was a member, a very active member, of the Ancient Order of Hibernians here in Boston, but that's not unusual. So far no complications . . . .'

He breaks off and finishes the whiskey, beckoning to the waitress who is serving the tables for another round.

'What's Mrs Cooney's angle in all of this?' Meryl asks, a trifle impatient.

'This,' replies Gene, picking up a photostat from the open folder. He doesn't give it to Meryl; he flourishes it like a courtroom lawyer as he continues his tale. 'Initially, Mrs Cooney took it that her husband had been killed in an accident, though she had nagging doubts. Apparently her husband said something to her which she didn't quite understand just two days before he died. He mentioned Washington and said he might have to go there soon to do some business. That puzzled her. In all these years he had never been to Washington and she knew of no connections that he might have there. Anyway, there wasn't enough in any of that to make her unwilling to accept the official account of her husband's death. Not yet anyway. The investigation, as you might expect, was handled locally by the Boston cops, her husband's own colleagues. But some time afterwards she had a visit from the Feds.'

'The FBI? What did they want?'

'This is where it gets interesting. And murky. Oh

36

thanks . . . .' The waitress is back with the drinks and she sets them down on the table. 'Keep the change.'

'Thank you, and have a nice day.'

'Here's looking at you kid,' says Gene in a moment of theatrics, raising his glass.

'Okay Humphrey. So could we just stick to the facts.'

'Aren't you pleased to see me?'

'Sure I'm pleased to see you.'

'So how about dinner?'

'Could we discuss that later,' Meryl tells him, though she is pleased he has mentioned it. 'You were about to tell me about the Feds . . . .'

'I thought you were a romantic.'

'You're the second person to say that to me today.'

'Who was the first?'

'My sister. She 'phoned from Cincinnatti.'

'Well, I mean it.'

'Will you get on with the damn story.'

'Sorry. Where were we . . . .?' He can't resist teasing her. He never could.

'The Feds.'

'Oh yes. This is where it gets a bit strange. The FBI called on Mrs Cooney and after pussyfooting around for a while they finally asked if her husband had left any unusual documents in the house.'

'And had he?'

'Not that she could recall.'

'What kind of documents?'

'That's the thing. When she pressed the FBI agents for more details, more specifics, they backed off and talked vaguely about "official papers" and crap like that.'

'And is that it?'

'No. The best part comes next. After the visit from the FBI Mrs Cooney is naturally enough curious. She's wondering what's cooking and, of course, her suspicions about the circumstances of her husband's death are once again aroused. So she starts a search of the house and goes through all his old things and finally – this is some considerable time after the FBI boys have been to see her – she discovers at the back of a bureau a small diary. And this' – he flourishes the photostat – 'is what she finds.'

He pushes the document across to Meryl. She takes it up. It is a photocopy of a single page measuring seven inches by three. The writing, small and crabbed, is clearly legible. So is the date: 21 July 1969. Meryl reads the following: 'Document is hot. Must take precautions. Belfast will want to know. The man in Washington can help. Will talk to Sammy MacAllen in NY first. He'll make the decisions. Chappaquiddick will be remembered for more than Mary Jo Kopechne. Kennedy is ahead of the posse. I wonder who in Dublin knows about the deal? Lynch must be in on it. It couldn't work otherwise. Holy Mary, what am I into? Must keep this from Mary. Must protect her. Things could turn very sour.'

Finkleheim waits, his face intent, his gaze focused on Meryl.

She looks up. Their eyes meet.

Silence.

He thinks he can see her thoughts forming.

'I need a cigarette,' she blurts out.

'Is that all you have to say?'

'Jesus, I don't know what to say. This is fucking heavy stuff. You know what I mean?'

Finkleheim picks up his glass and smiles. He's pleased with himself. 'I know exactly what you mean.'

'What's your guess about the document. The Kennedy document?'

'I think we need more than guesses . . . .'

11

FLASHBACK: The party at the Lawrence Cottage is beginning to break up. Somebody – was it Rosemary Keough? – is singing 'South of the Border' when Teddy Kennedy emerges from the bathroom zipping up his fly. He looks tired but he's grinning. His face is flushed, but it's hard to tell if he's pissed. He's not a heavy drinker, though eveyone knows he's knocked back a few. So what? Damn it, it's a party after all.

At the door of the cottage Mary Jo Kopechne has her coat on. She's waiting to go. Teddy has offered to drive her. He has taken the keys for the black Oldsmobile from his chauffeur, Jack Crimmins. Mary Jo needs a lift to catch the ferry going from Chappaquiddick island to Martha's Vineyard, a larger island off the heel of Cape Cod.

It is just 11.57 pm. Teddy is talking to Esther Newberg, one of the six girls in the cottage and one of his brother Bobby's campaign workers in 1968. He waves to Mary Jo to indicate he's on the way and kisses one of the other girls – Maryellen Lyons – on the cheek. She blushes.

At the door he shouts goodbye to Paul Markham, picks up his briefcase, takes Mary Jo by the arm and steps out into the darkness. To get to the ferry he will have to cross the Dike Bridge over the Chappaquiddick River.

The rest, as they say, is history.

When the story breaks it's a page one lead everywhere. Here is how the opening paragraphs in *The Boston Globe* account on 20 July 1969 read:

"EDGARTOWN – Sen. Edward M. Kennedy, the only

surviving brother in a family pursued by tragedy, narrowly escaped death early yesterday when his car plunged into a pond on a sparsely inhabited island off the coast of Martha's Vineyard.

"A passenger, Mary Jo Kopechne, 28, of Washington, a former campaign worker for the late Sen. Robert F. Kennedy, was drowned.

"The car went off a wooden bridge, turned over and sank to the bottom of Poncha Pond.

"Police say the accident occurred between midnight and 1 am yesterday on Chappaquiddick Island, where Kennedy was visiting with friends at a small cottage.

"Staffers for Robert and Edward Kennedy had been having a reunion there.

"Police Chief James Arena said last night that he will go to the Edgartown District Court tomorrow to file an application for a complaint charging Kennedy with leaving the scene of an accident without making himself known . . . ."

There is, however, a second and untold story. In truth, there may be several untold stories concerning Chappaquiddick, but there is one which concerns this narrative and which must be related.

Police Captain John Cooney is in Edgartown precinct station when Teddy Kennedy's Oldsmobile is brought in from Poncha Pond. Cooney is a big man, a tough old-fashioned cop who is shortly to be transferred on promotion to Boston.

The station is buzzing with talk of the Chappaquiddick incident. Reporters have arrived in droves and by this time it is the topic of conversation all over Massachusetts and indeed right across the States. This latest brush with death by the last of the four Kennedy brothers causes US radio and television stations to

40

interrupt live coverage of the Moon shot to broadcast a newsflash.

Cooney's chief, Dominick James Arena, comes into the room. He is carrying a transparent plastic bag with some of Miss Kopechne's personal belongings, and a water-sodden briefcase. He hands the items to Cooney. 'Put those on my desk, John. I'm gonna have to take a look-see in that briefcase just to check it out. First though I gotta 'phone Washington. The shit is really flying. Where are those god-damn statements? Must be outside in the patrol car. Be back in a minute, John . . . .'

He goes out and closes the door. Cooney hesitates. The briefcase has the initials 'E.M.K.' The urge is irresistible. The case has two straps and no lock. He undoes the straps and lifts the lid. The water has soaked through, but the papers inside are in plastic folders. Three of them. He has them halfway out of the case when he sees the heading on one of them. His breath whistles out from him.

'Ker-ist, what is this?'

He throws a furtive glance at the door.

The heading stares back at him from the open brief-case: 'THE KENNEDY MANIFESTO – Outline Proposals for the Settlement of the Northern Ireland Problem'.

A smaller, separate sheet of paper is stapled to the document. The typed message on it reads: 'Copies to be sent to The White House; 10 Downing Street, and The Office of the Taoiseach, Leinster House, Dublin. To be marked "Eyes Only".'

Cooney, now very excited, makes his mind up.

He pulls out the plastic folder with the Kennedy document, pushes the others back after a glance – one has a heading about relations with South Africa, the other has something to do with over-spending by the Pentagon – closes the briefcase and puts it down on

41

Chief Arena's desk alongside the plastic bag with Miss Kopechne's things.

He unbuttons his tunic and slips the folder inside. In the outer office the Chief's voice is audible. Cooney straightens his tunic and makes a conscious effort to relax. His heart is pounding . . . .

Four hours later he is sitting in a room he uses as a study in his home in another part of Cape Cod. The door is locked. The desk lamp is switched on, and the plastic folder is resting on the blotter in front of him. It takes him twenty minutes to read the eleven-page 'manifesto' typed in double-spacing.

When he is finished he leans back in the chair, disbelief etched on his face.

He decides to read the document again. First, though, a stiff whiskey is called for.

As a precaution, he will hide the document later on inside a grubby copy of *Hustler* magazine, where it will rest between the exposed breasts of a Hollywood starlet and the ample *derriere* of a stripper from Atlantic City.

The next day – after a virtually sleepless night – Captain Cooney makes an entry in his diary and shortly afterwards calls a man in New York. He is given very precise instructions at the end of a long conversation. Nobody is to be told of what has transpired.

Two days later, having complied with his instructions from New York, John Cooney is drinking with friends in a bar on Beacon Street in Boston. It is his day off and he's in civvies.

An hour and thirteen minutes later he leaves the bar, walks west along Beacon Street, and starts to cross over to the other side at the junction with Fairfield Street.

He never makes it.

The brown Pontiac hits him from behind, tossing him high into the air. He is dead before his body reaches the ground. His back is broken. *Requiescat in pace.*

12

The Lubbocks' Diaries – Extract Three:
The trouble with cars, I always say, is that they are lethal weapons. Still, I suppose we're stuck with them. Drive carefully. That's the motto. Especially on bridges. After all, how will it look in the history books if Edward Kennedy never makes it to The White House because of Chappaquiddick? Not that what the history books say really matters. It's just one version. The 'official' version – yes, I'll grant you that. But don't make the mistake of confusing 'official' with 'true'. Take the case of Ireland. I know a bit about the place because I've been giving it some attention of late. Now it has been my experience that where Ireland is concerned some accounts of 19th century history, in particular, would leave you with the impression that there was never a formidable and highly organised constitutional movement for change. The impression conveyed is one of physical force only. Maybe that's because the historians are male – most of them anyway. B. B. Bachinski made that very point to me the other day. She talked about guns as the expression, demonstration and imposition of a phallic authority. Maybe we need a knickerbocker history of Ireland? Or would that be too 'subversive'?

13

Meryl cogitates. There is much to cogitate about. Finkleheim waits, poking at the bowl of an empty pipe. He knows he has done his best to fit the pieces together, to lay it all out in front of her. And he's actually feeling chuffed.

They are still in the spacious bar of the Park Plaza Hotel, with its sombre, old-world decor and superb cocktails.

He reaches into his pocket for a tobacco pouch, and Meryl glances again at the photostat.

One thing has been settled: they are going to have dinner together.

Finkleheim waits, working on his pipe with deft fingers.

Meryl sighs gently.

'What's bothering you?' Gene enquires, breaking the silence.

'That damn document.'

He shrugs. 'I don't have all the answers – yet.'

She looks at him sharply. 'You said we need more than guesses. Do you have something more definite in mind? What does it all add up to anyway?'

He holds back, wanting to get his pipe right. For the first time since his arrival he seems relaxed and at ease. 'Your second question is the cruncher. I could be profligate in terms of speculation, but I'm not sure that would get us very far. So we'll leave that for the moment, until we have something more solid, more substantial. As to your first question, well, I did two other things before coming here and I think we have a new lead as a result.'

'Why didn't you say so?' exclaims Meryl, with a

touch of indignation.

'I'm taking it a stage at a time. It's the only way I know how. On reflection I decided we needed to know more about our cop friend, Cooney, now sadly deceased, and also his friend in New York, one Samuel MacAllen . . . .'

'What did you come up with?'

'A – that Cooney was not only a member of the Ancient Order of Hibernians, he was also involved in the American IRA network; and B, that MacAllen is similarly involved only higher up. A pal in the NYPD confirmed this.'

'MacAllen is known to them as an IRA man?'

Finkleheim nods. 'Very well known. Or at least he was . . . .'

'Why are we saying *was* – is he dead too?

Finkleheim nods again. 'I'm afraid so.'

'Oh shit!'

'My thoughts exactly.'

'It's not a bit funny. That document would make a great story. We'd have an exclusive on our hands. But why has it never surfaced? We're talking about ten years after all.'

'What do you think yourself?'

'I think the mere fact it existed even back in 1969 is the basis for a story in itself. If we could stand that up . . . .'

'Supposing something else happened?'

'Such as?'

'Assuming the document was important in the first place – and Cooney's reference to it in his diary as "hot" would tend to bear that out – then there is a number of possibilities.'

'Name them.'

'It could have been re-stolen, suppressed, destroyed or . . . lost.'

'Lost?'

'Why not? It's a possibility.'

'A very far out possibility, I should have thought.'

'You might be wrong there. Stranger things have happened.'

'Do you know something I don't?'

'I know lots of things you don't.'

'Fucking MCP!'

'Now, now, let's not rush things . . . .'

14

FLASHBACK: In the summer of 1972 the following events took place at a large, ultra-modern and very expensive office-apartment-hotel complex on the banks of the Potomac in downtown Washington.

'Hold it down!'

James McCord speaks in a loud whisper.

The Watergate building is familiar to him, but tonight he is nervous. This isn't like him.

Earlier in the day he spoke to Charles Colson at the White House. And Colson was nervous.

Maybe it is time to cut our losses and abandon the scheme, McCord suggests.

No. Colson is firm. Adamant. Get on with it.

McCord wonders if President Nixon knows.

He must.

According to Colson it is Nixon who wants the document.

The break-in is underway – the first of two break-ins at the Watergate complex, though it is the second that everyone talks about for the simple reason that on the second occasion the burglars got caught. It occurred on 17 June 1972 and forms the opening scene of Woodward and Bernstein's *All the President's Men*. Nevertheless, there was an earlier break-in on 27 May 1972, also mentioned in that book.

On this first occasion McCord has two others with him and they are under instructions to look for and steal several kinds of material from the headquarters of the Democratic Party inside the building.

Top of the list is anything that might embarrass Teddy Kennedy, still being talked of as a Presidential candidate despite Chappaquiddick three years earlier. Also any material that might besmirch the Kennedy family, particularly anything that might link the late President John F. Kennedy, or his brother Bobby, with the death in August 1962 of Marilyn Monroe.

McCord has also been told that there is one document the FBI are very interested in, except Nixon wants to get his hands on it first. A document prepared in great secrecy by Teddy Kennedy relating to Northern Ireland.

In the White House those close to Nixon even know he has a pet theory. He believes what happened at Chappaquiddick was no accident. Somebody tried to kill Kennedy.

McCord learns this from Colson.

'The Boss is going fucking loopy,' he remarks in disbelief.

Colson feels the same.

Yet Nixon remains convinced.

'Some son-of-a-bitch knows about that document. It's important. I can feel it in here, in my gut. Find it for me. Use the FBI. Use the CIA. I don't give a fuck. Just find it.'

McCord and the other two burglars are successful. At least they get in and out of the Watergate complex wsithout being caught. Next time McCord won't be so lucky.

But they find nothing. No trace of the Kennedy document on Northern Ireland.

'Zilch,' he tells Colson from a telephone a short distance from the Watergate building.

'Balls!' exclaims Colson.

He knows Nixon's rages.

15

Ms McClone is sitting in J. C. Hillery's Bar on Boylston Street. Before her on the table stands a glass of Jim Beam and a pack of Virginia Slims. Spread in front of her is *The Boston Globe*. It is 12.18 pm and she is waiting to have lunch with Alfonso Seagull. Right now he's on the way back from the Massachusetts Institute of Technology over in Cambridge at the other side of the Charles River where he's been attending a symposium on "Theatre, Technics and Mental Equilibrium".

The previous night while she was having dinner with Finkleheim, the call came from Alfonso. He would be in Boston by midnight. Apparently the invitation to the symposium was a last minute one.

'Can we meet when I get in?' her lover asks.

'No,' she tells him, thinking of Finkleheim.

'Why?'

'I have things to do.'

'I see.' He sounds disappointed.

'Why don't we meet for lunch?'

'Okay – you got it.'

An early night will do them both good, she thinks,

as she rejoins Finkleheim. He doesn't ask who the call was from. He has always shown remarkable restraint. She admires him for that, among other things.

J. C. Hillery's is doing a good lunchtime trade. It's a bar she's very fond of, a favourite haunt of reporters, gossip-columnists, artists and glamorous society ladies.

Alfonso Seagull enters.

They kiss.

'How was MIT?'

'Like the world of academe everywhere – boring, pretentious and self-absorbed.'

'I take it then you didn't enjoy yourself.'

'The event had its moments. And one can always learn something in situations that are not to one's taste.'

'You sound as though you've been reading Louis Auchincloss.'

'Good English is not the prerogative of the ruling classes.'

'Did you miss me?'

'Of course,' replies Alfonso, stiffly.

'How goes the play?'

'Fine. Well, not so fine, but we're getting there. How is your work coming along?'

'So-so,' she tells him, gesturing with her hand.

'Are you planning to go to Dublin to interview Lynch?'

'We may decide to do that. We have loads of material on him, but the resignation has changed the perspective a bit so it may be necessary to go and talk to him.'

'Let me know about that. I just might go along myself. I'd like to meet him. Anyway my project depends on your project . . . .'

'What do you mean?'

'I haven't told you yet but you are going to be in my play; you and Finkleheim. How is he anyway?'

'He's fine. He's on his way to New York. I'm going to join him there later.'

'How interesting.'

'Are you jealous?'

'Not a bit.'

She throws him a disbelieving smile. 'He was here last night.'

'Finkleheim?'

'Yes.'

'What are you two up to?'

'Not what you think. We may be on to something really sensational.'

'Can you tell me about it?'

'Not now,' she replies shaking her head. 'What's this about me being in your play?'

'It's you, or perhaps it's not you. There will be at least two characters called "Meryl McClone" and "Gene Finkleheim". I'm working on the basis of Gore Vidal's theory of the simultaneity effect as outlined in his novel *Duluth*.'

'I haven't read *Duluth*.'

'You should. You must. It's scurrility and wit are a large joy. It has sparkling prose and is stunningly imaginative with a whole warehouse full of special effects.'

'So tell me about this theory.'

'Vidal argues that the fictive law of absolute uniqueness is relative. He says that although each character in any fiction – as in any life or non-fiction – is absolutely unique, the actual truth of the matter is more complex. When a fictive character dies or drops out of a narrative he or she will then – promptly – reappear in a new narrative, as there are just so many characters and plots available at any given time. He calls this the "simultaneity effect" – it means that any character can appear simultaneously in as many fictions as the random may require. Anyway, I'm just adapting and expanding this in an attempt to break down or bridge the barriers between art and life. It's what I talked about this morning at MIT. Mind you, I felt it was over their heads a bit . . . .'

Meryl's expression suddenly changes. Pensive, she reaches for a cigarette. 'Strange you should say that . . . .'

'Why?' asks Alfonso Seagull, perplexed.

'Something happened last night when I was watching television in my hotel room – either that or I had a very vivid dream . . . .'

'What are you talking about?'

'I know it sounds crazy, but I appeared – me – in part one of a television series called "An Easter Prizing". I was playing the part of a Countess . . . .'

'Holy shit!'

16

FLASHBACK: Credits roll.

AN EASTER PRIZING
Part One
Written and directed by B.B. Bachinski

FADE IN –

Patrick Pearse turns to James Connolly.

'Who's doing the script?' he asks.

Connolly shrugs. 'I think I heard someone mention Paul Schrader.'

'That fellow who did "Taxi Driver" and

"Mishima"?'

'It looks that way.'

'But he's murder. He's bloodthirsty. He's a sadist. He's going to have us all killed. Don't you know that?'

Connolly shrugs and goes on rolling his joint. Thomas McDonagh passes by riding a bicycle and wearing a white dress, low-cut. Over in the corner of the spacious yard Joseph Mary Plunkett is practising "Honky-Tonk Woman" on the mouth organ.

'You got us into this,' Connolly says at last. 'What the fuck am I doing here. All I ever wanted was my own chipper in Phibsboro, but you – you wanted to be big in Las Vegas with your name up in lights and all that crap . . . you and Elvis . . . .'

'Don't start that again. All I said was forget about the fucking chipper and think big.'

'And setting fire to this place is your idea of big – Jesus!'

'It's a brothel.'

'It's The Purple Palace.'

'Does that mean it's not a brothel?'

'It means it's one hell of a fucking pain reliever . . . .'

'You know, you disgust me at times. And what is more you have no feel for the English language . . . .'

Pearse is interrupted in mid-sentence by the appearance of a statuesque woman wearing thigh-high red boots, matching hot-pants and a silver see-through blouse. In her hand she carries a silver coiled whip.

Connolly releases a low wolf-whistle. 'Look at those mammaries . . . .'

The woman is Countess Constance Markievicz.

FADE OUT

52

17

Dr Ernst Lubbocks is sipping tea. Inside the spaceship *Zintanza* all is going well. It is heading west, following a course for Las Vegas. A rendezvous in Nevada, in the desert between Reno and Vegas has been arranged.

'Interventionists,' proclaims Doctor Lubbocks, 'that's what we must become. Marx was wrong about history. There are no immutable laws.'

'Quite so,' agrees Ludmilla Erebus, who looks ravishing.

'Are all the details seen to?'

The blonde nods and smiles. 'Yes. Everything is arranged in accordance with your oders.'

'Good.' He consults a digital clock on the console. 'We must be ready to beam him up very soon.'

'I must say I'm looking forward to meeting him,' comments the girl with enthusiasm.

'And so you shall, my dear, always remembering of course' – he knows Ludmilla is big on bondage and s-m techniques in general – 'that we require him for a specific assignment.'

His voice has grown stern. He cannot abide foul-ups.

'I won't forget.'

'Good girl.'

'. . . and afterwards?'

'That's another matter.' The voice is less harsh. 'You shall have your reward,' he informs her.

The delight is visible on her lovely face. 'Oh goodie . . . .'

'Now stand by. That's Vegas off to our left. We'll be over the area any second. Okay . . . I have him on monitor. Steady. Let's beam him up . . . .'

The blonde throws the beam-up switch.

They turn around.

Behind them the doors of the beam-up chamber, properly called the 'Transporter Facility', have opened automatically.

A man steps out.

He is wearing faded blue jeans, cowboy boots, and a light pink shirt.

It is Steve McQueen.

'Hello Steve, my boy,' calls out Doctor Lubbocks. 'Glad you could join us. We need your help.'

Beside him Ludmilla Erebus has started to fidget with excitement.

'This is my assistant, Ludmilla Erebus. Come over here and say hello to her. She's been dying to meet you.'

Steve McQueen approaches, hand outstretched, his tanned face creasing into that knowing, cynical smile, the smile of one who has seen it all before. Ludmilla is weakening at the knees.

'Hiya, honey.'

She is aware that McQueen has the reputation of being a fantastic lover.

Already, as he takes in her lithe figure encased in the black catsuit, he is horny.

Doctor Lubbocks is starting to worry.

18

FLASHBACK: The Oval Room in The White House. President Nixon is pacing up and down on the blue carpet with the famous American Eagle woven into it together with the motto *E pluribus unum*.

Nixon looks tired and haggard. John Dean, counsel to the President, is waiting in the background. The two men standing next to the Presidential desk are Patrick Gray III, Director of the FBI, and Lt. Gen. Vernon Walters, Deputy-Director of the CIA. They are both distinctly ill-at-ease.

Nixon is angry.

'Is there no good news at all for me?'

Nobody replies.

Dean, his hands in his trouser pockets, looks down and scuffs the richly tufted carpet with the toe of his shoe.

'What about the New York end?' asks Nixon. 'Did your people come up with anything?' He is looking directly at Gray. The FBI Director looks disconsolate. He is shaking his head. 'No, sir. I'm afraid not.'

'What in the name of fuck is going on? You have all these resources and all you can do is come here and tell me you can't help me. What the fuck good is that?'

Silence.

'John, what do you make of this?'

Dean looks up at the President. 'We're having a run of bad luck, sir.'

'You can fucking well say that again. Wasn't there some talk of a woman? Didn't this guy – what's his name? Mac-something-or-other – have a woman on the side. Some kind of mistress?'

The FBI Director glances at Lt. Gen. Vernon Walthers, a plaintive look on his face. 'That's correct, sir,' says the latter. 'We believe Sammy MacAllen did have a mistress.'

'What do we know about her?'

'Not much. The word is she's a black. And a hooker.'

'A black whore.' Nixon seems genuinely surprised.

'Who is she? Where is she?'

Walthers grimaces. 'We don't know, Mr President. Not precisely. We're still trying to pin that down.'

'Try harder. You're no fucking good to me otherwise. I need the document – do I maker myself clear?'

19

Jack Lynch puffs on his pipe. He has been talking now for nearly an hour, talking about his life and times, his background, his sporting career, his entry into politics, his ministerial career, and his period in office as Taoiseach.

Alfonso Seagull sits listening intently, taking copious notes.

'On St Patrick's Day, 1957, I was working in my office in Cork and I got a 'phone call to ring Dev who asked me to come and talk to him next time I was in Dublin. I went to see him as arranged and he offered me Gaeltacht or Education. I got on well with Dev and liked him a lot . . . .'

Seagull pauses to open another can of Budweiser, Lynch is wearing a charcoal-grey suit, white shirt, and a dark red tie. His mood is effusive.

'. . . Naturally the promotion to Finance fuelled speculation that I would be the successor of Sean Lemass as leader of Fianna Fáil and as Taoiseach. Quite early on, as the speculation mounted, my wife and I discussed the prospect and we concluded definitively that I should make it clear from the outset that I would not be a contender for the position . . . .'

The playwright has forgotten the Christian name of Lynch's wife. He makes a note to remind himself, another *aide-memoire*.

'Of course the North was to be perhaps my major preoccupation as Taoiseach. The Northern situation gave a new dimension to the position of Taoiseach because for the first time, at least in our generation, the words one spoke could have resulted in the loss of lives of fellow countrymen in the North. I was careful to pursue a consistent political line throughout on my handling of the Northern situation. At the Fianna Fáil Ard-Fheis in January 1969 I said: "The first aim of Fianna Fáil today is to secure by agreement the unification of the national territory" . . . .'

Seagull is anxious to get to the Arms Trial of 1970.

'Remember what we had been through over the previous four years. There was a time during that period when it was widely believed we would be decimated at the polls whenever an election took place. This was of course largely due to the dismissal of Ministers on May 6, 1970 and the resignation of another minister. Naturally this was a very trying period for me personally. Although I was not close socially to any of the people involved, I had grown up in politics with them. To have had to dismiss them from office was a very painful thing to do as was the subsequent recrimination. History will adjudicate on the rights and wrongs of that period but I felt I had no option but to act as I did, given the information placed at my disposal by the security forces. There have also been suggestions that I orchestrated the prosecutions throughout the affair, but again the fact of the matter is that I had no involvement whatsoever in anything to do with the prosecution or with the conduct of the case once I handed the papers over to the Attorney General . . . .'

Lynch pauses to light his pipe which has gone out. Seagull is impressed by him, and reckons he now understands better the point which Meryl McClone has made emphatically to him in the past, namely, that behind the rather gentle, avuncular exterior and the soft-spoken façade there lurks a steely presence.

There is much more to come. Seagull consults his watch. It must wait. He puts aside the half empty can of beer, gets up, goes across and switches off the video recorder. A third of the tape is still left. Later. Seagull wants to see part of another tape. Both have been given to him by Meryl. He wonders where she is. After lunch in J. C. Hillery's she gave him the tapes and then left him. One of the things she said she had to do was book a flight to New York.

As he changes the tapes he recalls her account of what she saw on television – or dreamed she saw – and he begins to ponder Gore Vidal's theory.

Are we in the realm of the occult? he asks himself. He pushes the question aside. He has work to do, a commitment has been made to deliver a script. A deadline must be met.

Seagull switches on the new tape and retrieves his can of Budweiser.

On the television Meryl McClone is talking to Gene Finkleheim about Jack Lynch.

20

The two men have been watching her for some time. In fact they have been tailing her ever since she left J. C. Hillery's Bar in Boylston Street. She never saw them there, being far too preoccupied, nor did she notice when one of them deliberately walked past her table to get a closer look at her.

He liked what he saw.

Now Meryl McClone is down near the end of Cambridge Street, close to Longfellow Bridge. She knows she has disappointed Alfonso Seagull by leaving him after lunch. She knows he wanted her to go back to the hotel with him, and to bed. Post-prandial trysts are a speciality of his, suggesting to her that he has Latin blood somewhere in his veins. This, she decides, is a fatuous thought and unworthy of her.

All she wants just now is to be on her own for a while, to occupy her own space, and to sort out her thoughts. The video tapes will keep Alfonso happy for a while: he's really wound up over this new play.

She stops just short of the river and decides to search out a bar. For the past hour she has wondered aimlessly, much to the annoyance of the two men shadowing her, and now fatigue is setting in. The thought of sitting in a quiet corner of a bar with a cool drink is appealing.

She settles for a place called "The Three Masts".

Inside it is dark and quiet. Perfect. The place has a strong aroma. She decides it is a combination of floor polish and rum. The bar has a polished timber floor and old ships' storm lanterns hanging from the ceiling.

Meryl orders a glass of beer. As it is being served two men enter. She doesn't see them. She is seated at the counter on a high stool, her back to the door.

One thought keeps recurring. Is there something to be found in New York, or is she and Gene Finkleheim on a wild goose chase?

The beer is cold and refreshing. She notices the two men. They have come to the counter to order. They are young, in their mid to late twenties, and soberly dressed. When she takes a cigarette from her handbag one of them reaches across and flicks a lighter.

'Allow me.'

She glances casually at him. He is quite good-looking. 'Thank you', she murmurs, bending forward to avail of the flame.

Drinks are served and the barman moves away.

'Do you know Boston well?' the young man with the lighter asks. His colleague averts his eyes. It seems to Meryl there is a trce of a mid-European accent in the man's voice. She can't be sure.

'I know it fairly well,' she replies evenly, 'though it isn't my home town.'

'We wondered if you knew someone we are looking for. We're strangers here . . . .'

'I don't know that many people here. Some, but not many. Who are you looking for?'

The young man's gaze is steady. His eyes are blank, his face closed, expressionless. Almost. 'We are looking for a man named Lubbocks. Doctor Ernst Lubbocks.'

Meryl hesitates, not because she knows anyone of that name but because it has suddenly dawned on her that this conversation may not be as fortuitous or as innocent as she thought. Call it women's intuition.

Two pairs of eyes are staring at her.

Little fingers of unease are creeping up her spine.

'I don't know anybody of that name,' she tells them, even-voiced.

'Are you sure?'

'Quite sure.'

'Do you know a woman named Bachinski?'

'No.'

'A tall blonde, very attractive. A sexy lady, always dresses in black.'

'I don't know her,' insists Meryl, a tightness now discernible in her voice.

'Are you sure?'

'Of course I'm sure. What is this anyway? Who are you?'

A ghost of a smile flickers across the face of the young man next to her. 'Let's just say we're interested parties.'

'Interested in what?'

'In the same thing as you and your partner.'

Meryl is nonplussed. And they know it.

The two men withdraw.

'We'll be seeing you.'

At the door one of them turns, the one who has done the talking. 'Miss McClone,' he adds, very deliberately, like a line from a play.

They exit.

Meryl is transfixed to the stool.

Jesus, they know about Gene and me: they know my name.

Fear grips her and it is intensified when she suddenly remembers the name 'Bachinski'.

The writer-director of 'An Easter Prizing' was called B.B. Bachinski.

Meryl McClone feels vertiginous, lost, confused, forlorn and afraid. All at once.

21

American Airways Flight 378 for New York is airborne. Gene Finkleheim watches Boston receding rapidly below and behind him. His thoughts are already on New York and on what he hopes to find there.

The arrival in Boston of Alfonso Seagull is a complication he – and, he suspects, Meryl – could have done without. Still, she can come on to New York later. That's what they've agreed.

He settles back in the seat. The aircraft is less than one-third full. He has chosen an aisle seat on the very back row. It's an old superstition of his which he can't shake off.

A hostess goes by, all white gleaming teeth and ruby-red lips, and he orders a drink.

New York is one of his favourite cities; he loves its buzz and its electric atmosphere. It is a city of which or in which he has never been afraid. This time it could be different. Momentarily he broods and is instantly annoyed with himself. Brooding is something he is not much given to. Yet he has always been rich in imagination – it is an invaluable trait in a journalist – and he knows that those with vivid imaginations see more clearly and starkly than others the evil, the perfidy and the inhumanity of the world, the dark and frightening recesses where lurk the psychopaths, the tyrants and the sadists.

The drink arrives and he is grateful for the intrusion. The disturbing train of thought is broken. Very deliberately he turns his mind to the woman he is leaving behind in Boston.

It is some minutes later when it happens. His hand, he thinks, must have strayed onto a button in the armrest. He's not sure. Not of that. What he is sure of is that a screen came down in front of him and he is suddenly and disconcertingly staring at himself.

His face – it is his unmistakably – stares back at him through rolling credits announcing

AN EASTER PRIZING
Part Two

FADE IN
James Connolly scratches his head. Over his right ear.

He is quite bald.

The Countess goes past, all eyes turning.

'What a woman,' remarks Connolly. 'Want a drag?' He offers the joint to Pearse.

'No thank you,' replies the latter, stiffly.

'The trouble with you is that you don't know how to relax.'

'I prefer a Decade of the Rosary any day. Why do you smoke that stuff?'

'It blows my mind.'

'You mean your alleged mind . . . .'

'There's no need to be nasty. Your turn will come.'

Plunkett puts away the mouth organ and ambles over. 'Somebody gave me a white rose but I don't know what I did with it.'

'I thought red was your colour,' suggests Connolly.

'No. That's this geezer,' replies Plunkett, indicating Pearse. 'Have you ever seen his underwear?'

'At least I'm not like that pervert McDonagh, going around in the Countess's clothes . . . he's bonkers . . . .'

'She's all right, though,' muses Plunkett, who is feeling horny.

'Who?' asks Pearse, innocently.

'The Countess. Did she ever show you her tits? Wow – what a pair!'

'I don't know which of you is worse – you or Connolly.'

'He likes her tits too – don't you, Jamsie me boy?'

'I fancy that mother in a big way.'

'But does she fancy you – that's the zinger, isn't it?'

'What's a zinger?' Pearse wants to know.

Plunkett rolls his eyes in disbelief. He knows Pearse is thick, but this is ridiculous. 'It's what you get when a titled lady puts her snow-white hand on your rollers . . . .'

Connolly starts to laugh and nearly swallows his

joint.

Pearse blushes.

'I'll tell the Countess what you said.'

Plunkett is staring into the mouth organ, one eye closed. 'She already knows,' he says with a sly smile and winks at Connolly. Connolly winks back.

'You mean you . . . .' Pearse's face goes puce. It's a common condition for him.

'We're surrounded by perverts,' pronounces Plunkett.

FADE OUT.

The screen goes blank and then it disappears.

Finkleheim doesn't move. All he can do is blink.

He blinks again.

To his left the tall towers of Manhattan, that familiar skyline featured in a thousand Hollywood movies, comes into view.

'We thank you for flying American Airways,' intones a female voice over the aircraft's intercom,' and on behalf of Captain Lubbocks and the crew . . . .'

Finkleheim blinks again.

Finally, he bestirs himself and tentatively reaches out his right hand and grasps his left wrist. He holds it and squeezes and waits, as though reassuring himself that he is still real.

He is, believe me.

22

Alfonso Seagull is worried. Where the hell is Meryl?

He plucks nervously at the lapel of the denim jacket he is wearing. It has a 'Ban the Bomb' badge attached.

Meryl is late. Very late. And that's not a bit like her.

Seagull is tired of sitting around, tired of Jack Lynch, tired of Ireland and tired of being a radical playwright. All he wants now is Meryl and her curvaceous body with its clearly defined and familiar erogenous zones.

Where is she?

Moments earlier in the bathroom as he freshened he was on the verge of masturbating. No, he decides, that would be a waste.

He wants to look for her, to find her, to hold her, to fondle and caress her. And then to fuck her.

The problem is she isn't here and he doesn't know what to do.

J. C. Hillery's.

It comes to him as he is contemplating the bulge in the front of his jeans.

Meryl's favourite pub in Boston. Yes.

To Boylston Street.

Seagull rushes out, forgetting to lock the room behind him. On the coffee table are the two video tapes given to him by Ms McClone.

He leaves the hotel and walks at a fast pace through the slush, oblivious of the cold. As he rounds Boston Common and heads into Boylston Street he spots a newstand. The vendor is stocking copies of *Gambit*, a theatre magazine he has been looking for. The current issue has an extended profile of the British playwright, Howard Barker, one of his favourites. He must have a copy.

He hurries on, head down, glancing quickly through the pages. The Barker piece is there all right. J. C. Hillery's is halfway along Boylston, on the right-hand side as you approach it from the Boston Common end. As he walks Seagull shakes off some of the erotic obsession which has gripped him. His desire for Meryl, he tells himself, must never again be all-consuming. Howard Barker has done this to him. Made him ashamed. Barker's writing opposes all obsessions. And Barker is one of his heroes.

In J. C. Hillery's he finds her at the far end of the bar, huddled in a booth with red leather seating, smoking pensively and sipping a large whiskey.

When he enters she looks up, startled, wide-eyed.

'What is the matter?' he asks.

Meryl McClone is mute. She turns away and picks up the whiskey.

'Where have you been?'

She swallows a sizeable amount and grimaces.

'Do you hear me?'

'I was . . . walking . . . .'

'Walking? Didn't you know we had an appointment?'

'Yes.'

'So what happened?'

'I walked.'

'Did you forget?'

'I did, I suppose. I'm not . . . sure . . . .'

Seagull sits down. He starts to reach out a hand to her but pulls back. 'You know, I'm sitting back there with this hard-on for company, waiting for this vision of a broad to walk through the door and jump on my bones and . . . .'

Meryl explodes.

'Oh fuck it, Alfonso – don't you ever think of anything else when it's me?'

He is taken aback.

'Hey, come on now,' he says placatingly. 'This is Alfonso Seagull remember? Soul-fellow, friend, mentor, pal, lover. It's me, sweetheart. You know me. I'm not some ogre.'

She glances at him sheepishly, knowing she has overreacted, but also knowing that he doesn't know what has happened to her.

'I'm sorry . . . I'm sorry . . . it's just . . . .'

'It's just what?'

'I met these two guys.'

'When? Here?'

'No. A little while ago. More than a little while ago, I guess. In a bar.'

'Have you been cruising the Combat Zone again?'

Meryl gives him a come-off-it smile. She knows he's trying to be funny, teasing her. The 'Combat Zone' is Boston's red light district close to Boston Common and back of Tremont Street.

'Are you going to talk to me? Tell me what happened.'

She draws on her cigarette and then stubs it out. 'I'm scared, Alfonso. I think they were secret agents.'

'Secret agents.' The incredulity vibrates through his voice. 'You mean like the CIA or the KGB . . .?'

Meryl nods her copper-haired head.

'Are you sure?'

Her head shakes. 'No. I'm not sure of anything anymore, except that I'm scared . . . real scared . . . .'

23

The Lubbocks' Diaries – Extract Four:
American Gothic – that's my theme. Violence, paranoia, dementia. Come to think of it, it's Irish Gothic as well. Nightmare visions, crosses and gravestones, broken bodies and rivers of blood. I see a landscape littered with burnt out cars, shattered buildings, shards of glass, and a brooding simmering hate that threatens to engulf us all. Out of this wreckage, heavy with the rancid smell of

putrefaction, the flies buzzing in hordes above the corpses, rides a lone figure on a horse. On his head is a black stetson, and over one eye he wears an eye-patch. The horse, head down, is showing signs of fatigue, the rider's dark green shirt is covered in dust and ashes. The one good eye stares straight ahead, unwavering, determined. The features are drawn, lines of tiredness down both cheeks. Up close the likeness is unmistakable. It is Jack Lynch on horseback. In the background a signpost says 'Belfast'. Up ahead a man is waiting. He unholsters a Colt .45 and breaks it open. All six chambers are full. He spins the cylinder and resets it, dropping the gun back into the dark leather holster. He is not a tall man and his face is dominated by an over-large nose. Thin blue veins are visible on it. Ask his name and he will say: 'Call me Charlie, though some call me "The Boss".' Others claim his name is Haughey. The word is he's deadly fast. He waits, watching the approaching rider. Charlie is good; he has survived numerous shoot-outs. But this is the showdown he has been waiting for. In the saloons he has passed the word along — 'I want Big Jack'. Even the dancing girls are aware of what he's planning.

The rider is close now.

The one they call Haughey steps directly into his path.

'Draw!' he barks, right hand poised.

The rider keeps coming.

'Draw, damn you!'

Nothing registers on the face of the one-eyed rider. His countenance is like carved granite. It's as if the other man isn't there.

He keeps coming.

At the last moment Haughey has to step aside.

The rider goes past, facing into the setting sun.

It's not over yet.

24

East 106th Street is on the edge of Harlem, very definitely a no-go area for whites these days. Finkleheim knows this. He knows New York. You don't go unescorted into Harlem anymore, and even then you don't go without a damn good reason.

He reckoned he had a damn good reason. The best. A good story. Or oblivion.

Most of the faces around are black. Finkleheim stops the hired Chevrolet and does a quick look around. This is not his territory and he would prefer not to be here. If there was any other way . . . he knows there isn't.

Soon it will be piss-or-get-off-the-pot time. Very soon. He decides he's going to piss.

The trouble is Meryl may have something to say about that.

He checks his watch. It's time to be getting back. He u-turns the Chevy and heads back down Eighth Avenue heading along Central Park West. Over the 'phone he and Meryl have arranged to meet in a bar off Columbus Circle. When they talked she was aspprehensive and recounted what happened in 'The Three Masts'. He isn't altogether surprised though he doesn't admit this. Things are starting to get dirty.

'Look after yourself,' Meryl tells him before hanging up. He's mulling this over in his mind as he approaches West 59th Street. A large billboard is advertising a production of Sam Shepard's 'True West' on Broadway.

It switches his mind to Alfonso Seagull. That bastard is getting in the way, he tells himself. Or maybe I'm just jealous. Jesus, I haven't even 'phoned

Janine. She'll be furious. Why must women be so uncomprehending at times?

Correction. Change that to 'some women'. And the exceptions? Put Meryl McClone at the top of the list. And it's not just her tits I'm thinking of. At the thought of those splendid mammaries – what a vulgar word 'tits' is – Gene Finkleheim permits himself what can in all honesty only be described as a phallocentric smile.

The owner of the objects which prompted that smile is waiting for him. Punctuality has always been a thing with her. When he goes to kiss her she responds with warmth. Meryl hasn't kissed him like this in ages.

Well . . . .?' He invests the word with both surprise and a query.

'I just missed you.'

'I'm glad. And also sorry I wasn't there.'

Their eyes meet.

'Could we try that again?'

Meryl smiles and shakes her head. 'Let's keep it for special occasions.'

'That sounds reasonable.'

'Tell me what's been happening.'

'Let me get a drink first. Will you have another?'

'Yes, please.'

'Bartender, the same again for the lady and I'll have a Jack Daniel's on the rocks.'

He pulls a stool up and seats himself. 'On the way here I saw your television saga . . . .'

'My television saga?'

'Okay – let's call it *our* television saga.'

'You mean . . . "An Easter Prizing"?'

'That's exactly what I mean.'

'Were you in it?'

'Oh yes, and well I looked too even if I say so

myself.'

'God, it's not funny. Not one bit. What do you make of it?'

Finkleheim shrugs. 'I don't know . . . .'

'Then I wasn't dreaming?'

'I never thought you were.'

'Can minds really connect? You know, mental telepathy or something like that? ESP?'

The drinks arrive.

'I wouldn't rule it out,' Finkleheim concedes. 'Anyway, here's to us.'

'Yes. I'll drink to that.'

'You look lovelier than ever.'

When she glances at him she sees the earnestness of his expression. 'Thank you, kind sir.' Slightly disconcerted at the new current of feeling running between them, she turns away to search for a cigarette. Finkleheim picks up a book of matches from the bar counter and lights it for her.

'Thank you.'

He sits watching her, his eyes partly hooded.

'Do you think someone is trying to tell us something?'

'Maybe.'

'A warning?'

'Perhaps. I just don't know.'

Meryl looks sombre.

'Do you want to go on with this?' Gene asks.

'I just don't want to back away . . . but I wish to Christ I knew what was going on . . . .'

Finkleheim, pensive, sips his whiskey. 'Perhaps the answer is up in Harlem.'

25

An item from Ireland is coming over the UPI wires:
'The battle to succeed Jack Lynch as Prime Minister of
the Irish Republic is already underway. According to
informed sources in Dublin the main contenders are
Charles J. Haughey and George Colley . . . .'

26

'Is this it?'
   'Yes.'
   'What now?'
   'Drop me at the next corner.'
   'Then what?'
   'Drive around. Give me ten minutes and pick me up
here again.'
   'Will you be okay?'
   'Sure.'
Meryl McClone brakes and brings the Chevy to a
halt alongside the kerb. Gene Finkleheim gets out.
They are at the corner of Lenox Avenue and 135th
Street in the heart of Harlem. After a quick glance left
and right he walks quickly into the bar just around the
corner. As he does so the Chevy pulls away from the
kerb.
   Neither of them has spotted the blue Dodge
Charger lurking in the darkness. It has tailed them
from Columbus Circle.
   Inside the bar Finkleheim turns down the collar of
his overcoat. The girl is waiting for him at the counter,

wearing the light blue mini-dress she described over the 'phone. 'I take it you're Rona?'

'I sure am, honey.'

Rona is tall, slim, beautiful and very black. She wears an Afro hairstyle.

'Light me.' She flourishes a cigarette. Finkleheim searches for matches.

'What's the deal?' she asks as he shows her his Press card. Rona gives him an appraising look over her cigarette and blows smoke in his face. 'Damn it, don't do that.' She laughs, displaying a perfect set of teeth. The dress is low-cut and Finkleheim is having a hard time keeping his eyes off her cleavage.

'It's a daiquiri for me, honey,' she tells him, eyeing her empty glass.

Finkleheim, his eyes watering, snaps his fingers. A black face glares at him from behind the counter. 'A daiquiri and a Jack Daniel's on the rocks. Please.'

Rona is mocking him with her eyes. They are hazel.

'Sam said you would help me.'

Sam is Finkleheim's friend, a reporter on *The New York Times*.

'Sam is right. But it'll cost you, honey.'

'How much?'

'Five hundred bucks. Upfront.'

'Okay.' He reaches into his trouser pocket, pulls out a bundle of notes and peels off five hundreds. Rona, cigarette dangling from crimson lips, stuffs the money down her cleavage.

'You wanna go now?'

Finkleheim checks the time. 'Finish your drink. There will be a car outside in two minutes. Do we have far to go?'

'Naw. Four blocks.'

A man approaches. Rona smiles at him. 'Later, honey,' she tells him, knowing what he wants. 'I gotta

73

go out for a spell. Set up some drinks and I'll be back real soon.'

He turns away without a word. He is middle-aged, well-dressed and white.

'Who was that?' asks Finkleheim, uneasy.

Rona flashes her teeth. 'One of my regular tricks, man. Whitey likes black pussy. Of course you know that – or are you different?'

The hazel eyes mock him again.

'Can we go?'

'Sure, honey,' says Rona, crushing out her cigarette. She flounces towards the door and he follows.

At the kerb outside the Chevrolet is waiting. They climb in.

'Where to?'

'Go to the junction of 140 and Eighth,' instructs Rona, settling back in the seat.

Meryl McClone eases the Chevy out into the traffic, heading North, deeper into Harlem.

As they pull away from the sidewalk the blue Dodge Charger follows keeping well back.

FLASHBACK: A bar in West 42nd Street, across the road from the office of *The New York Times*.

'The word is Sybil disappeared,' says Sam, the reporter from the *Times*. Finkleheim is listening intently. 'What happened?' he asks.

The reporter hunches his shoulders. 'Who knows? She could be in Mexico. That was the word for a while. Somebody said she was running a cathouse in Tijuana. She could also be at the bottom of the East River with an engine block tied to her feet . . . .'

'Cheerful,' remarks Finkleheim, giving his pal a twisted smile.

'That's me.'

'So it's another dead end?'

74

'Maybe not. I'm told her closest friend and the only person she really trusted is a black hooker who operates out of Harlem. Name of Rona. Here, I have her telephone number. Tell her you were talking to Sam.'

Finkleheim arches his eyebrows.

'Strictly business,' adds Sam, grinning.

'Apart from making all my fantasies come true, what else can this Rona dame do for me?'

'If Sybil left town in a hurry – or disappeared into the East River – she wouldn't have taken luggage with her. She would have left her stuff with Rona. They used to share an apartment. Maybe they still were when the heat came on and Sybil split.'

'So Rona still has most of her stuff?'

'That's what I'm told.'

'It's worth a try.'

'Yeah. Give it a shot. What have you got to lose?'

'You mean apart from my trousers . . . .'

27

Steve McQueen opens a can of Coors. He is sitting in the recreation room of the 'Zintanza' watching a video of himself in 'The Magnificent Seven'.

It's the scene early in the movie where he and Yul Brynner offer to drive the horse-drawn hearse up the hill to the cemetery.

'Watch this,' shouts McQueen, excited. 'Watch the top window.'

Ludmilla Erebus stretches langorously. She is sitting on the armrest of McQueen's chair, the zip of her black catsuit pulled down to reveal sizeable segments of her braless breasts. She is also very bored having had to sit through three McQueen movies. This is the fourth and he hasn't even kissed her.

'It's just another horse opera,' she tells him. 'Why can't we put on some music and dance?'

McQueen, genuinely startled at her bland comment on what he regards as one of his greatest films, turns to glare at her. But before he can say anything the voice of Doctor Lubbocks comes over the spaceship's intercom.

'Steve, can you come to the control deck right away. Our friends need your help. It's time to beam you down . . . .'

28

'Where is she?' asks Finkleheim as Rona gyrates to the sounds of Sonny and Cher's chart-topping version of 'I Got You Babe'.

'Who?'

'Your pal, Sybil?'

'Gone, man. Long gone.'

'Where to?'

'She didn't say.'

'Even if she had, would you tell me?'

Rona halts. She confronts him, her eyes bright, the pupils dilated.

This black bitch is wired on drugs, Finkleheim is thinking.

'I might, honey, if the price was right.'

'Is she dead?'

'Shit, man, why you go and ask that?'

'Well – is she?'

Rona's expression changes. 'I dunno,' she replies, low-voiced.

'What about her stuff? Can we take a look now?'

'Okay with me. It's all in here, though there isn't much.'

Finkleheim follows her into the bedroom where there is a tall mahogany wardrobe. Rona opens it and pulls out an old red and white TWA bag. She unzips it, takes out an assortment of undergarments, some dresses, trinkets and a pair of red shoes with long spiky heels. Sybil's working gear, Finkleheim muses as he watches. Rona throws the clothes on the bed. She picks up a flimsy pink panties with a heart embroidered on the crotch.

'Nice – huh?' she says, giving him a teasing smile.

Finkleheim ignores her. 'What else is there?'

'Come see for yourself, honey. . . .'

He takes the bag and turns it upside down on the bed. 'Is there another bag?'

Rona shakes her Afro hairstyle. 'That's all there is. Sybil wasn't one for keeping stuff. Just her favourite things.'

'Does that include raunchy reading?' asks Finkleheim, pulling old copies of *Playboy* from the bottom of the bag.

'Sybil was in *Playboy* once. She used to be a model, you know . . . .'

They're all models, Finkleheim tells himself. 'What about *Hustler* – was she in that too?'

'Naw,' answers Rona, picking up a sequinned mini-dress. 'She never mentioned *Hustler*.'

Finkleheim glances at the cover of the magazine. It is dated July 1969. He tosses it aside and it spills open on the bed, spreading a naked body across the bedclothes. His eyes follow the nude photographs. There is something else. Something protrudes from the pages. A document.

He reaches for it, excitement and anticipation gripping him. He pulls it free of the nudes. A quick look at the front page tells him what he wants to know.

He has found *The Kennedy Manifesto*.

Wide-eyed, he turns the pages skimming the contents. Rona, nonchalant, sits on the bed and smokes.

'Jesus Christ,' he exclaims as he reads.

She looks up. 'Was it worth five hundred bucks?'

Finkleheim beams. 'You bet – and thanks.'

'Don't thank me yet, honey,' she tells him, turning towards him and reaching for his fly.

'What are you doing?'

'You paid me five hundred bucks, didn't you?'

'Sure . . . .'

'I gotta do something for you in return. Something special.'

'But I've found what I'm looking for . . . .'

'Fair is fair,' she says firmly, her slim fingers pulling his already semi-erect penis free of his trousers.

'But . . . listen . . . .'

'Don't argue with me, honey,' she instructs as she bends and opens her crimson lips to receive his manhood.

'Can we hurry this up,' sighs Finkleheim resignedly.

Rona is too busy to reply.

29

Along West 57th Street in the centre of Manhattan two middle-aged women emerge from a pharmacy. A man passes by on the other side.

'My God!' exclaims the first women. 'That's Steve McQueen.'

'Don't be silly,' comments the second. 'He's in Hollywood.'

'Didn't he die?'

'I'm not sure . . . .'

30

The Lubbocks' Diaries – Extract Five:
Why do men do it? Why do they thirst after power and why are they willing to do anything – or almost anything – to acquire it? Is that what politics has come to? I've been considering that in the Irish context, not least because Jack Lynch is on my mind. The physical force brigade is to the fore again. One question keeps resurfacing – look at all the 'hard men' and ask yourself: did they ever experience a childhood? Think about it.

31

James Connolly rolls a joint.

Meryl McClone blinks.

It's happening again, she thinks, momentarily unmindful of Gene Finkleheim and Rona.

History is unmaking itself before her eyes. Cultures collide. And time itself loops and warps.

As she waits in the Chevrolet Meryl is watching a television through the window of a bar. The 'Easter

Prizing' saga rolls on.

Connolly pulls deeply on the joint and glances at his script. 'Do I have to say this?'

The glass, the concrete, the distance make no difference. Meryl can hear every word.

B.B. Bachinski is angry. This is not the first time there has been hassle over the script. And it's already been rewritten twenty-two times. The director's patience is running out. Time is money. Real time, that is. And time is being wasted. 'Will you please – just this once – not fuck about.'

'It's easy for you to say that but I have to think of my new image,' protests Connolly.

'Image!' screams Bachinski. 'You want cosmetics and I'm offering you cosmic greatness.'

'Is there a difference?'

'If you have to ask that . . . .' Bachinski is close to despair.

'Forget I said it,' says Connolly placatingly, knowing he has gone to the limit.

'From the top, please,' instructs the director, tersely.

Meryl McClone, still watching the screen, gropes for a cigarette.

James Connolly consults his script and straightens his shoulders. 'In the beginning was an island,' he intones, 'and the island was with us and we did not care. And some mad god said: "Let there be strife." And they came on pale-green horses, coming down from the mountains and across the plains. At a place called Tara the goddess Magdha bestirred herself, covered up her nakedness, and proferred a golden chalice of wine. Behind her sixteen white-veiled virgins plucked on harp strings. "This is for the peacemaker," proclaimed Magdha. "Let him step forward." The serried ranks parted. A man stepped forward, diffident, balding. "Who is this?" asks

Magdha. "He is a southern chieftain, O Great One," replied one of her acolytes. "He is called Lynch." Magdha sniffed. "Give him a horse and send him forth. Then let us retire to the mead-hall . . . ".'

'Cut!' shouts Bachinski.

FADE OUT

32

As Finkleheim zips himself up the fellatrix tends to her lipstick.

She is good, he thinks.

'Satisfied honey?' inquires Rona, lighting a cigarette.

'Absolutely,' nods Finkleheim, not quite sure whether she is referring to her own prowess or to the discovery of *The Kennedy Manifesto*.

'I give value for money.'

'You sure do. Now can we get out of here?' He is thinking of Meryl waiting outside in the Chevy and of what has to be done next.

'Grab your stuff and let's go.'

They exit but not before he has taken the precaution of reinserting the Kennedy document between the pages of *Hustler*. It has proved a safe hiding place up to now and may do so again.

Out on the street Meryl finally manages to divert her attention from the television screen, now carrying images of Sammy Davis Jr in an advertisement for coffee.

Three hundred yards away, lights dimmed, the Dodge Charger moves slowly forward closing the gap with the Chevy. Meryl remains unaware of its presence. Nothing else on the street is moving. Not yet.

Ms McClone stubs out her cigarette and glances anxiously towards Sybil's apartment. The Dodge is closer now.

A door opens. Finkleheim and Rona emerge, the woman click-clacking after him in her spiky heels and tight dress.

Further up the street another door opens. A man in a black fedora steps from the Dodge, a .38 Smith and Wesson in his right hand.

Meryl reaches across to unlock the offside doors.

'Hold it, you two!'

Finkleheim turns first and sees the man with the gun.

Rona has frozen.

'Run!'

It's another voice, another man, coming out of the darkness across the street from the Chevy.

Meryl, unsure of what's happening, reaches for the ignition key.

The man from the Dodge Charger is looking across the street at the intruder. His partner in the car switches on the headlights, flooding the street with brightness.

'Get to the car!'

Finkleheim grabs Rona by the hand. 'Come on!'

Meryl, panicking, can't get the car to start.

The man with the gun swivels back to the two figures rushing towards the Chevy.

'Halt!'

'Don't stop,' shouts the man who has come from the shadows. He is closing fast on Meryl's side of the Chevy.

A gun blasts.

Rona falls.

'Christ!' Finkleheim swears.

The figure in the street pulls a gun and squeezes off a shot. It goes wild slamming into the wall above and to the right of the crouching figure from the Dodge. But it forces him to drop to the sidewalk.

Finkleheim bends over Rona. Her bosom, no longer heaving, is already covered in blood.

'She's dead.' It is the man from the shadows who makes the pronouncement, his hand on her temple. 'Let's get the hell outa here.'

They run for the Chevy.

'Shove over,' the man from the shadows tells Meryl. 'I'll drive.'

'It won't start,' she exclaims in terror.

'Move over.'

'Jesus!'

Meryl is staring, mouth open. The man who has taken her place behind the wheel is Steve McQueen. He pumps the accelerator, jerks the ignition key and the engine fires. Behind him Finkleheim has thrown himself across the back seat. McQueen guns the engine and powers the car away from the kerb, keeping his foot down as he executes a u-turn.

In the street a gun flashes. No contact. The man with the Smith and Wesson scrambles aboard the Dodge Charger.

McQueen works the gears, the Chevy accelerating along Eighth Avenue, the Dodge giving chase.

Alongside him Meryl, not yet over her amazement, can only think of the wild car chase sequence on the streets of San Francisco in 'Bullit'. She is both scared and exhilarated.

McQueen, reading her thoughts, grins boyishly. 'Yeah,' he hisses. 'Only this time it's for real, baby . . . hold on . . . .'

33

'Three beers, please . . . .'

Finkleheim pays and walks back to where McQueen is sitting with Meryl. 'That was close,' he remarks, setting down the glasses.

'No, it wasn't' replies McQueen coolly. 'They were just amateurs.'

The car chase didn't last long. At Cathedral Parkway McQueen sent the Chevy into a power slide that took it into Amsterdam Avenue almost on two wheels. The Dodge Charger tried to emulate the feat but, lacking a Steve McQueen, it ended up going through the plate glass window of a furniture showroom.

Meryl stares at McQueen, an unlit cigarette between her fingers.

'Where did you come from?' asks Finkleheim, who had to wait until the Chevy stopped outside the bar in Columbus Circle before discovering the identity of the driver.

McQueen smiles enigmatically. 'Let's just say a friend sent me.'

'Say "thank you" for me when you get the chance,' Meryl tells him.

'Will do,' he says, fixing his blue eyes on her. She feels herself beginning to blush. Finkleheim doesn't notice. 'What about Rona?' he asks.

'Who was she?'

'A hooker,' he tells McQueen.

'Somebody will send for the meat-wagon. It happens here all the time.'

'What happens?' asks Finkleheim.

'Hookers get killed almost every day in this town.'

'She helped us.'

'So did I.'

'We're grateful,' Meryl tells him. He smiles at her again and sips his beer. 'What next?'

'We need to get this out of New York,' explains Finkleheim, unfolding the copy of *Hustler* magazine he took from the apartment in Harlem.

McQueen gives him a 'come-off-it' look.

'Not the magazine,' Finkleheim adds. 'This.' He pulls out *The Kennedy Manifesto*.

'You got it?' interjects Meryl, in what is a half-question and a half-statement. She is clearly delighted, the ardours of the past hour forgotten for the moment.

McQueen gives the document a cursory glance. He doesn't really care what it is. 'It's important, is it?'

'Yes. Very,' says Finkleheim emphatically.

'The other crowd – is this what they are after?'

'Yes.'

'Who are they?'

Finkleheim hesitates; he is afraid that if McQueen is told the full truth he may not want to help them any further. And they need his help. 'We're not sure . . . .'

McQueen grins, his eyes closed to slits. 'Never mind, we're the good guys and they're the bad guys. That's enough for me. What's your next move?'

'We need to get this document out of here,' repeats Finkleheim.

'Where to?'

'To Ireland.'

Meryl, remembering what happened to Rona, interjects. 'We need to get ourselves out of here.'

'Yeah,' agrees Gene, his mind elsewhere.

'What about authentication?' asks Meryl. Finkleheim looks up sharply. 'What do you mean?'

'I mean how do we prove the document is what we say it is?'

'I haven't read it in detail, but what I saw tells me it has the ring of truth about it – or at least the ring of credibility.'

'That might not be good enough,' insists Meryl.

'What do you suggest? We can't ask . . . .' He hesitates to use the name 'Kennedy' in the presence of McQueen, knowing the former's ties with the Hollywood set. 'We can't ask the man himself.'

'Maybe not. But what if we could find somebody who is, or was, close to him at the time?'

'Do you have someone in mind?'

'I do,' replies Meryl.

'So?'

'Let me make a 'phone call.'

34

At around the same time in another part of Manhattan a man in a black fedora is using another 'phone. 'They got away . . . I'm sorry . . . a third party intervened . . . some guy . . . I don't know . . . I thought he looked familiar somehow, but I can't place him . . . . they gave us the slip on the corner of Central Park West . . . .'

The man on the 'phone pauses, listening to the voice at the other end. He is the man from the Dodge Charger, the man with the Smith and Wesson, the one who killed Rona. He makes no mention of that over the 'phone. He is also the man who spoke to Meryl McClone in 'The Three Masts' in Boston.

'I'm not sure . . . he was carrying something in his hand when he came out . . . we must assume so . . . .'

He listens again. The voice at the other end is talking about options.

'If we are to cover all of them then we will have to think in terms of Ireland . . . yeah, it's where it would make the greatest impact, particularly now . . . that's my thinking exactly . . . .'

When the call is finished the man in the black fedora breaks the connection, rings the operator and asks for an overseas number. He's unsure of the time over there, but it doesn't bother him. His instructions are clear – ring whenever there is news, day or night.

The operator comes back.

Belfast is on the line.

35

On board the *'Zintanza'* Doctor Lubbocks pours himself a cup of tea. Ludmilla Erebus is standing by. They are both wearing headsets. He indicates a second cup on the tray. Ms Erebus shakes her head. Tea is not her favourite beverage. The Doctor sips his and removes the headset. 'Did we tape that coversation?' he wants to know.

The girl nods. 'Yes, it's all on tape.'

'Good.'

They have been eavesdropping on the calls made by the man in the black fedora.

'Just as a contingency measure, I suggest we plot a course for Ireland.'

'Will we be taking Mr McQueen with us . . . .'

The doctor raises his eyebrows.

'. . . if we go, that is?' adds Ms Erebus.

'I expect so.'

Ludmilla's lovely face creases into a smile, and Doctor Lubbocks casts his eyes heavenwards. He is uncertain about the precise nature of McQueen's gifts *vis-a-vis* women, though there is no disputing he has them. Or it.

The Doctor sighs inwardly and turns his thoughts to Ireland.

36

Alfonso Seagull puts aside *Gambit* magazine and conjures up his favourite image of Meryl McClone. He is troubled and in need of solace.

Sitting in a taxi on the way into Manhattan from La Guardia Airport, it seems to Seagull that Meryl is embarking on a project which may take her out of his life and back into Gene Finkleheim's. In other words, he's jealous. Damn right.

In additon, he's beginning to feel that his own project, 'The Green Ayatollah', is running into trouble. So far it hasn't jelled, and he knows it. This leaves him edgy and a little sour.

There was a time not so long ago when all he wanted from Meryl McClone was her body, a night in the sack together. Not anymore. Now he wants a commitment, a declaration of love, even marriage. He wants it but is afraid to even broach the matter lest he be rejected. And he's not at all sure he can cope with rejection.

He knows she and Finkleheim lived together once. He has always known. From the beginning Meryl made no secret of it. It was all over, finished, a closed episode belonging to the past. Or so he thought.

Not anymore.

That's what he fears – that and artistic failure or artistic stasis. A dreadful kind of impotence. Self-doubt is beginning to eat at him. Like a lover of whom much is demanded, or who demands much of himself, he is beginning to wonder if he can deliver, if he can live up to the (self-imposed?) demands.

Meryl McClone has told him where she is staying in New York. He desperately wants to see her – she is now, he tells himself, both his personal and artistic saviour.

And she may not even want him. The thought emboldens him.

I'll kill Finkleheim, he resolves, slapping the back of the driver's seat so hard that the cabbie looks around anxiously.

'Sorry,' mutters Seagull, feeling sheepish.

I'm beginning to crack up. It's all Meryl McClone's fault. She never should have shown me her tits. They are my downfall. Christ.

Sinatra's voice fills his head. 'If I can make it there, I'll make it anywhere; it's up to you, New York, New York . . . .'

It's fucking easy for Sinatra.

37

'There's no doubt about it.'

'Are you sure?'

'Yes.'

'But did you ever see the document?'

'No.'

'You never actually saw it?'

'No. But I was asked by the Senator to do research for it. I even prepared a first draft.'

'Did that include stuff about NATO bases and

facilities in Ireland and economic aid if these were conceded?'

'Oh yes, they were the central propositions.'

'Even then?'

'Yes. Even then.'

'Did Senator Kennedy ever say where the idea came from – you know, the idea of trading economic aid for NATO bases in Ireland and US backing for a United Ireland?'

'We discussed it once. He left me in no doubt it came in part from a very prominent Irish politician . . . .'

'Which one? Did you know?'

'I was never told directly.'

'But you knew?'

'I surmised.'

'But you were close to the action?'

'The signals pointed in a certain direction.'

'So who was it – was it Jack Lynch?'

'Like I said, I was never told directly. But I always understood it was Jack Lynch. It could have been someone else.'

'Wow – what a story!'

Meryl McClone and Sheri MacFerson are sitting on a bench in Battery Park, looking out over the Hudson River. In the distance, out in the bay, they can see ships passing the Statue of Liberty.

They had met once before, back in the early seventies when Ms MacFerson was still on Senator Kennedy's staff in Washington.

'Can we prove any of this?' queries Ms McClone.

Ms MacFerson, a dark and petite woman of 36, returns her stare. She is a Radcliffe graduate and was highly respected during her Washington days. 'I can testify to the fact that I was engaged on behalf of the Senator in drafting a document which is not in essence dissimilar to the one you've described to me. That should help.'

Ms McClone looks away, staring sightlessly across towards New Jersey. At this stage there is no question of showing *The Kennedy Manifesto* to Sheri MacFerson or anybody else. In any event, Gene Finkleheim is most reluctant to allow it out of his sight. They have even talked, for reasons of security and safety, of posting it on ahead on a poste restante basis to an address in Dublin, one of the hotels perhaps, like the Shelbourne or the Gresham, which they both know. 'It should,' agrees Ms McClone at last, 'but will it stick?'

Ms MacFerson fishes out a pack of Kool from her handbag and offers one to Meryl. The latter shakes her head. 'I'll smoke one of my own.'

'Is it signed?'

Meryl recalls the very brief examination she has made of the document in the presence of Gene. They did it furtively while McQueen was in the men's room. 'No signature that I can remember. No, there is none. But the first page is typed on Kennedy's official Senate notepaper.'

'It's something, but not much. It wouldn't be too difficult to get hold of a few sheets of Senate notepaper from Kennedy's office. At least a dozen staff members have direct access to it, probably more.'

'When did you leave?'

'I left in 1973 to get married. My husband died two years later.'

'I'm sorry.'

'It doesn't matter now. It seems a long time ago.'

They exchange glances. Silence. Over towards Staten Island a ship's hooter sounds.

'You know, this is one of my favourite spots in Manhattan. I come here a lot,' says Ms MacFerson.

Meryl smiles thinly. 'I like it also . . . .' Thoughful, she draws on her cigarette, the breeze coming in from the river whipping the smoke away. 'Why would Kennedy have dropped the whole idea of the *Manifesto* on Northern Ireland?'

Ms MacFerson, eyes downcast, shrugs. 'I guess there could be any one of a number of reasons. Timing. Opportuneness. Feasibility. Acceptability. You must remember it was drafted in early 1969 – I did my version around mid-March I believe . . . .'

'Before Chappaquiddick?'

'Exactly. That changed a lot of things. Prior to that everything that Kennedy did was geared towards the 1972 Presidential Election.'

'Including the document on Northern Ireland?'

'Oh yes. The Irish-American vote would have been crucial to him, as it was to his brother Jack in 1960. And the Irish-American voters, the overwhelming majority of them anyway, would have seen no contradiction in attempting to trade NATO facilities in Ireland for economic aid and the promise of support for a United Ireland.'

'And Jack Lynch – how would he have viewed it, do you think?'

Ms MacFerson smiles bleakly and elegantly pouts. She is attractive without being a dazzling beauty and Meryl has warmed to her. 'It was 1969, remember. The situation in Ireland as I understand it – and we talked to Kennedy a lot about this, and to visiting Irish politicians as well – was very different then to what it is now. Also bear in mind that Lynch followed Sean Lemass as Prime Minister, and Lemass was the supreme pragmatist. He had gone North to meet Terence O'Neill, the Northern Ireland Prime Minister, in 1965 and he had spearheaded a new era of industrialization in the Republic. In 1969 the promise of more jobs and of substantial aid for the economy – North and South – might have taken the steam out of the whole explosive situation. At that time, and this is crucial, momentum on both sides was still coming from economic self-interest, not from ideology. Now it's very different. The ideologues have taken over; the extremists on both sides have come into their own. The moderates like Lynch, who wasn't blinded by nationalist sentiment and who saw the limitations of a politics of catch-cries and slogans – are largely *passé*. The ground has shifted, perhaps even dramatically, though it may be some years yet before we can gauge the extent of the shift . . . .'

Meryl is impressed and says so. 'Why was there – why is there – so much interest in *The Kennedy Manifesto*?'

'I think it's because there's still an element of mystery about it, and a belief that it might in some magic way have worked. A kind of Hibernian Holy Grail. Very few people know it exists, even now, and fewer still know its contents. Kennedy's enemies wanted it at the time and, presumably, still want it in the hope that they can find something in it with which to discredit him. He could still, after all, be the next President of the United States. Others want it for their own propaganda purposes, to make it serve their own ends.'

'How do you feel about it – the document, I mean?'

'Accepting that the document is along the lines you describe – and I haven't seen your version – I think there is a good deal of sense to it. I've always felt that way. And if you had a sufficiently hard-headed and pragmatic Prime Minister in Dublin, given the current economic climate in the Republic, I think it's a package you could sell to the people in the 1980s. I mean, why not? Most people are pissed off with the

93

Northern Ireland problem, the cycle of violence, and the way the whole thing is draining off energies and resources. And as for Irish neutrality, that's a sham anyway . . . .'

Meryl turns all of this over in her mind. 'You could well be right,' she muses. 'How do you feel about coming to Ireland?' The question is asked on impulse, and she has no idea how Finkleheim will react if Sheri MacFerson accepts.

'To publicise the document?'

'To help back up our story that it exists – and perhaps even to make a little bit of history. The network will pick up the tab.'

Ms MacFerson smiles and reaches out a hand to touch Meryl's. 'Why not.'

'Great,' exclaims Meryl who, even as she speaks, is aware that she has made no mention of the shooting in Harlem.

38

Back at the hotel Meryl finds two messages awaiting her. One is from Gene informing her that he has gone to make arrangements for their trip to Ireland. In a PS he tells her McQueen has 'left'. This disappoints Meryl. She was hoping he'd stick around.

The second message is from Alfonso Seagull. He's in town and intends calling around to the hotel in half an hour to see her. She greets this second message with mixed feelings.

Up in her room she kicks off her shoes, fixes a drink, lights a cigarette and switches on her Sony cassette recorder. It's time to put something on tape. No sooner has she started dictating than the 'phone rings. She picks up the receiver. It is Gene Finkleheim.

'I've done a deal to get us across by boat from Miami to Cuba,' he tells her.

'Cuba?'

'Yeah. Aeroflot operates a daily flight from Havana to Moscow via Shannon. We can get off there. It's our best bet. And they won't expect us to use Cuba. They can't stake out Havana Airport.'

Meryl sees the sense in this. Then she remembers Sheri MacFerson. 'You'd better make arrangements for three people. The Kennedy woman is coming with us.'

If Finkleheim regards this as problematic he doesn't say so. 'Okay. I've made reservations for us in Dublin at the Shelbourne, but I think you should keep that to yourself. And I've also airmailed the document on ahead, so that's out of reach. Treat that *sub rosa* as well. From here on in we can't be too careful.'

'Fine.'

'I have a few more things to do. See you soon. How about dinner?'

'When do we leave for Miami?'

'At midnight.'

'At midnight?'

'Yes. We cross by night.'

'I'm not wild about that.'

'It's safer that way.'

'Okay – if you say so.'

'How about dinner?'

'I'm . . . not sure. Alfonso is in town . . . he's coming to see me.'

'Oh shit.'

Meryl is secretly pleased by this reaction; she feels the old chemistry between herself and Gene is beginning to work again. 'Why don't you call me again later on, say in about an hour or so?'

'I'll do that. Either way I'll be there at midnight to pick you up.'

'See you then. Take care.'

'You too.'

They hang up. Meryl starts the tape again. She wants to say something about what Sheri MacFerson has told her. The words won't come. The reason is simple: her thoughts are very much on Gene Finkleheim.

Then she remembers Lucette. A trip to Ireland will mean being away for at least a week, and she was planning to go to Cincinnatti to spend some time with her sister.

Meryl, leaving the tape still running, picks up the 'phone and dials Lucette's number.

Lucette is out but her answering machine is hooked up.

'Hi, it's Meryl here. I'm calling from New York. I'm afraid I can't come to visit for a while yet. Gene and I have to go to Ireland at short notice. We're going down to Miami tonight and then crossing over to Cuba where we'll catch a flight from Havana to Shannon. It's somewhat of a circuitous route, but what we're doing is a bit hush-hush so it's the best course. If you need to get in touch we'll be staying at the Shelbourne Hotel in Dublin. Hope to see you in about a week or so. Love you, sis . . . .'

As she hangs up the doorbell rings.

It is Alfonso Seagull. 'Hello lover.'

Meryl stares at him.

'Don't I get invited in?'

Meryl steps aside.

Seagull walks in. 'Are you all right?'

Meryl closes the door. 'I'm fine.'

'You don't seem very pleased to see me.'

'Just now I've got a lot of things on my mind.'

'Including Gene Finkleheim?'

'Why do you say that?'

'It's starting all over again, isn't it?'

'I don't know what you're talking about,' retorts Meryl angrily.

'Oh come off it. You've got the hots for him again. I can tell.'

'Jesus, Alfonso, is that all you can think of?'

'It's true, isn't it?'

Meryl, exasperated, clenches her fists. 'Why did you come here, Alfonso?'

'What do you mean?'

'I mean what are you doing here?' As her blazing eyes focus on him, he averts his gaze.

'I want you.'

'Do you mean you want to fuck me? That's what you usually want, isn't it?'

'No, no – that's not what I mean . . . .'

'Do you want to fuck me, Alfonso? Is that why you're here?'

He looks at her but says nothing.

Meryl begins to unbutton her blouse.

'What are you doing?"

'Let's get it over with, shall we?'

Without another word he rushes for the door, slamming it after him.

Meryl stands perfectly still.

She can hear his footsteps pounding along the corridor.

Her thoughts are confused, all jumbled up.

Silence. No more footsteps.

Meryl redoes the buttons on her blouse and turns to look for a fresh cigarette. It's only now that she realises the cassette recorder is still on. She stops it, presses the rewind button, and plays back portion of the tape.

97

The severity of her own voice, its almost raucous quality, takes her aback.

Poor Alfonso. He deserves better. Maybe I am more than a good lay to him.

39

The Lubbocks' Diaries – Extract Six:

Passion is a terrible thing. Harness it to a gun and you have a recipe for mayhem. Alfonso Seagull knows that. He wrote a play once called 'Topless in Wichita' which was not at all what it seemed. It was about a man with a gun who in his passion for fame decides to start killing people. When passion rules reason flies out the door. That may not be very poetic, but it's true nevertheless. Arouse passion and turn it loose on the issue of nationalism and you have a recipe for social turmoil and communal bloodshed. That was another point in Jack Lynch's favour. He recognised that. Do many of us realise how thin is the membrane of ordered civilisation which is stretched over a world of social chaos and metaphysical uncertainty? Ask Alfonso Seagull about that sometime, but not now. At the moment he's a deeply troubled man. Passion. That's what it's all about, that's the cause of it.

40

'We're going all the way on this, aren't we?'

Gene Finkleheim nods. 'Yeah – I guess you could say that.'

'Why?' inquires Meryl. 'Can you tell me why? Do we know?'

'I could throw a cliche at you.'

'Like "a man's gotta do what a man's gotta do"?'

'Something like that.'

'I don't want that crap.'

Finkleheim spreads his hands, palms upwards. 'What do you want?'

They are sitting in a quayside bar along Baywater Boulevard in Miami, bags packed, waiting for a call. They're both drinking Bloody Marys. A third drink is on the table. Sheri MacFerson is in the ladies loo. Like Meryl, Finkleheim likes her; she's sharp and knowledgeable and not afraid to fight her corner. She'd make a good television producer, he decides. On the journey down from New York they've talked about politics and power, about journalism and history, about films and death.

No mention is made of Rona.

Otherwise the journey goes without incident.

'I want to know if we're getting in over our heads?' persists Meryl, who is in foul mood.

'I don't think so,' he says, after a long pause.

'Do you know the kind of people we're dealing with? Do you have any idea?'

Finkleheim purses his lips. 'Are you getting scared?'

'Not getting – I am scared.'

'Why?'

'Jesus, we're dealing with hatchetmen and you ask me why!'

'Once we get across to Havana everything will be all right.'

'You don't think we're safe now?'

Finkleheim looks directly at her. 'Look, Meryl, I don't know who's in on this. I just don't know. Some crazy things have happened, and it's not over yet.'

'Why can't we just back away from this?'

'Is that what you want after all this time?'

'What do you want? We'are just a couple of reporters – remember?'

'This is more than that – I know it.'

'More than what, for chrissakes?'

'We're into something here that goes beyond
journaliam . . . .'

'You sound like a fucking visionary or a zealot.'

'We're caught up in something really big – I can
sense it.'

'That's irrational.'

'Maybe it is, and maybe you wouldn't have always
thought so. We're always on the brink except most of
the time we're afraid to acknowledge it.'

'On the brink of what?'

'We spend most of the time in that very narrow zone
between rationality and irrationality or, if you prefer,
between history and imagination. You can compare
us to the snail on the razor blade Marlon Brando talked
about in 'Apocalypse Now' – never quite sure what is
rational and what is irrational . . . .'

'You're beginning to worry me, Finkleheim, with
all that metaphysical shit,' observes Meryl tartly,
opening her briefcase to get at the carton of Virginia
Slims she purchased before leaving New York. When
she lifts the cover of the case a photograph of Jack
Lynch and his wife Máirín stares back at her. They
both look at it.

'You know what some hot-shot editor in New York
is going to say of course – he's going to say: "Jeez, this
story needs sex appeal". You know how they think.
Nowadays every story has to have a blood, sex and
drugs angle. Otherwise it lacks hype. And without
hype baby, it won't sell – isn't that what they're going

to say?'

Finkleheim grins crookedly. 'We have a non-starter then . . . .'

'We can give them blood – lots of it.'

'Yeah, we can do that all right. The streets of Belfast are awash with it.'

'But it's thumbs down on sex. Lynch didn't play around.'

'I've been thinking about that, and of course you're right. This man played it all above board. There's never been even the merest hint of sexual scandal. That's another interesting thing about the man's character. He was not without guile, far from it. And he could be as tough as nails. I remember one time down in Cork talking to John A. Murphy, professor of history at the University there, and he said to me: "There is a fist in the glove, though the glove is very much in evidence". I think that's very true. Lynch was upfront most of the time. He could be devious, I think there's enough evidence for that. But there isn't much light and shade in his character . . . .'

'Chiaroscuro.'

'What?'

'Chiaroscuro. That's what the experts call light and shade.'

'Thank you,' says Gene, relieved to see Meryl's bad mood lifting.

'With Lynch what you see is what you get.'

'Precisely. No financial skullduggery and no sexual intrigue.'

'Boring, boring . . . .'

'That's what New York will think.'

'Fuck New York.'

41

The man behind the counter shrugs. 'Take your pick, buddy.'

Alfonso Seagull picks up a Magnum. 'Jesus, it's heavy.'

'Whaddya want – a water pistol?'

'I meant . . . I'm looking for something I can carry around without making me seem like the leaning tower of Pisa.' He is standing at the counter of a Miami gunshop, just five blocks from where Gene, Meryl and Sheri are waiting to be picked up.

'Why not try this Browning nine millimetre?'

Seagull picks up the gun. He is not a gun-person and it shows. He handles the weapon awkwardly. 'How do I load this thing?'

He watches as the owner of the store pulls the magazine from the handle of the gun, displays it, pushes it back in place and works the slide. 'Now you've got a shell in the breech – see, right here. She's all ready for action. You just pull the trigger and the other guy is dogfood.'

'How many bullets does it hold?'

'A Browning magazine holds thirteen shells.'

Seagull pulls a bundle of dollar bills from his pocket. 'I'll take it.'

'Want me to wrap it?'

'Yes. No – it'll do fine as it is . . . .'

'Suit yourself, buddy.'

Seagull is thinking of Meryl and of his own self-image as a writer. It's time for theory to give way to praxis, he tells himself with grim determination, clutching the new weapon. I've been a thinker for too long: now the time has come for me to transform myself into a man of action. You can call it the 'Hemingway Factor' if you like. Either way Finkleheim ends up dead.

42

The Lubbocks' Diaries – Extract Seven:
There is something in the male – perhaps in the female also, though it's a different syndrome – that is attracted and aroused by guns. I suppose it has to do with potency, with power and with phallilc symbolism. A little man becomes a big man if you give him a gun. And a man who can't cope or compete with the dominion of love may be seduced by the love of dominion when he discovers what a gun can do for him. Be warned. And remember that in another context Jack Lynch tried to abolish the guns; he tried to take the gun out of Irish politics – and failed. But he'll be remembered for trying.

43

It is only when it is over and they have left that Lucette is able to reflect and tell herself that they looked like a couple of Yale types.

Her blouse is torn open and the red blotches are still visible on her breasts.

She is no longer sobbing, no longer shit-scared. Just trembling and confused. This is her America after all.

So what is she doing here half-naked, her torn bra lying on the floor?

Tell me. Tell me just what the hell is going on?

Meryl.

That's who they want.

Why?

Her hands are shaking. She searches for a cigarette.

It is all on tape. The information. The message from Meryl about Miami, Havana and Ireland. All on the answering machine. The Yale types know all that now. And they're chasing Meryl.

Where is she? I can't even warn her.

Watch out Meryl. They're coming for you. I don't know why, but they're coming.

Lucette starts to cry.

44

In pre-Castro days it was the glamorous and raunchy Calypso Nightclub in the centre of Havana. Today it is a nightclub again but the name has been changed, the decor is suitably sedate and topless waitresses are no longer to be seen. The taxi, a battered Buick, drops Meryl, Sheri and Gene at the canopied entrance. They have four hours to go before their departure from Jose Marti Airport.

'A slice of Cuban life is what we need,' Finkleheim declares.

The nightclub is seedy, slightly delapidated and expensive. On stage a dusky Cuban *chanteuse* is singing 'The Way We Were', the house lights are dimmed, and most of the tables are occupied. At the end of the number there is polite applause, the house lights come on full, and the singer leaves the stage and begins to greet people at the tables.

Finkleheim is cleaning his spectacles when he feels Meryl going rigid alongside him. He replaces his glasses and follows Meryl's stare.

A man, small, stocky and bespectacled is talking to the *chanteuse*.

It is Alfonso Seagull.

He makes animated gestures and the singer looks around as though trying to locate someone.

Seagull is agitated. He grabs the girl by the arm and she winces in pain. He points towards the stage. The quartet of musicians are huddled in a corner enjoying a break and a drink. Seagull hurries to the stage. The *chanteuse* has put a hand to her face, uncertainty stamped all over it, perhaps even traces of fear.

The playwright, ignoring the musicians, picks up a microphone.

'I know you're here, Meryl. I followed you from Miami . . . .' His voice booms through the nightclub.

Meryl gapes in astonishment.

Finkleheim half rises out of his seat.

'You must get away from here,' Seagull shouts. 'They're on to you. Do you hear me?' His perspiring face glistens under the stage lights. 'Run for it, Meryl. It's your only chance. The bastards are here. Get away while you can. Please. I'll do my best to stop them . . . .'

He takes a gun from inside his jacket and brandishes it. 'I'll do anything for you, Meryl, but please run. Get away before it's too late.'

Meryl starts to rise, tears forming.

Finkleheim is back in his chair, exchanging wide-eyed stares with Sheri MacFerson.

A shot rings out.

Seagull staggers.

Two men come on to the stage from behind the musicians. They are carrying guns.

Meryl recognises them instantly. 'Alfonso!' she

screams, rushing forward.

A second shot.

One of the men falls, crashing against a cymbal. The other retreats, disappearing from view.

When Meryl reaches the stage Seagull is slumped over, bleeding profusely. Finkleheim and Sheri MacFerson are just behind her. People are on their feet all over the place, some pale-faced with fear, others screaming hysterically.

The *chanteuse* gets to him first, cradling him in her arms.

He looks up at Meryl. 'Go away please,' he whispers. 'Get to Ireland . . . .'

'Why in heaven's name did you follow me?'

'I wanted . . . to . . . protect . . . you . . . .'

'Who were those men?' Finkleheim asks.

'Shouldn't we get a doctor?' suggests Ms MacFerson.

'It's too late,' Seagull tells her, without self-pity. He smiles at Meryl. 'Do what I tell you – go away from here.'

'What about you?'

'I'm just switching to another play. This one's over . . . .'

'Oh shut up Alfonso . . . .'

And he did.

For keeps.

Meryl bends and kisses him.

Finkleheim is worried. 'Is there a back way out of here?'

The *chanteuse* points. 'Through there. And you'd better hurry. There's a taxi rank just down the street.'

Finkleheim helps Meryl to her feet: she has managed to hold back the tears. 'Are you okay?'

'I'm fine.'

'Let's go then.' He gestures to Sheri MacFerson.

'Good luck, you three,' says the *chanteuse*, as they move towards the backstage exit.

In the excitement they have forgotten her name, though she's billed outside the nightclub as 'the exotic Alana Leone'.

It's better this way, she tells herself.

45

Fidel Castro turns to Jack Lynch.

'Is it really true that you knew nothing about the plan to import arms until the 20th April 1970?'

'Absolutely,' replies Lynch, poking at his pipe.

'And the full story has been told?'

'My side, yes.'

'It wasn't a very good plan.'

'I wouldn't know anything about that.'

Castro pulls another cigar from the top pocket of his tunic. Behind his desk there is a large poster of Che Guevara side by side with one of Elizabeth Taylor. 'I would have shot them.'

'What?'

'I would have shot them.'

'Why?'

'For not telling me, number one. And number two, for making a balls of it.'

Lynch is shaking his head. 'Ireland is not a banana republic.'

Castro gives him an arch look. 'Are you sure?'

Gene Finkleheim shivers involuntarily and wakes up. His dream of Cuban-Irish dialogue vanishes. Meryl and Sheri are asleep on either side of him. The Aeroflot flight from Havana is two hours from

Shannon. Finkleheim has an unfinished drink in front of him. He picks it up and memories come flooding back of another drink in another place at another time.

FLASHBACK: He is in Mulligans of Poolbeg Street. Up at Doheny and Nesbitts in Lower Baggot Street Michael Mills, the political correspondent, is waiting for him. The talk in the pub is all about guns. It is the 23 October 1970 and just hours after the dramatic 'not guilty' verdict in the Arms Conspiracy Trial. From the cuttings Finkleheim knows that what is to pass into history as 'The Arms Trial' has its genesis in the outbreak of communal violence in Northern Ireland in late 1968 and 1969 and appeals by some representatives of the Northern Catholic minority for guns. This in turn leads to a decision taken on the 16 August 1969 by the Dublin Government to the effect that 'a sum of money, the amount and channel of disbursement of which would be determined by the Minister for Finance, should be made available from the Exchequer to provide aid for the victims of the current unrest in the Six Counties'.

Later, on the 18 March 1970, £100,000 is voted as a grant-in-aid for the relief of distress in Northern Ireland. This is the money which is used for the attempted importation of arms from Europe and after the failure of this plan two members of Lynch's Government are dismissed. One of the two men – Charles Haughey – is tried and acquitted.

In Doheny and Nesbitts Michael Mills is talking to a journalist from Fleet Street when Finkleheim comes in. 'None of the political parties in the Twenty-Six Counties was emotionally or strategically prepared for the problem created by the turmoil which broke out in the North in 1969,' explains Mills.

'Why was Lynch so slow to act?' asks the man from

108

Fleet Street. 'Was he uncertain or just weak?'

Another reporter, someone told Finkleheim later his name was Bruce Arnold, interjects. 'When we come in the future to look back on this period we will see Lynch as the reluctant man of power, doing the minimum and delaying it for as long as possible . . . .'

'Will he survive all of this?' the man from Fleet Street wants to know.

'Oh yes, definitely,' asserts Mills, in a judgment which proves sagacious.

Finkleheim is impressed. He feels at the core of great events, happenings which are shaping the destiny of a nation. Impressed but also troubled.

Does anyone have the full story? Does anyone ever have the full story where momentous events are concerned? He wants to ask the pundits around him, but the pub grows more crowded and noisy and the opportunity passes.

'That's history.'

'What did you say?' asks Meryl, waking up.

'I said "That's history".'

'What's history?'

'We are. Wittgenstein was right when he said: "Mine is the one and only world". History' – Finkleheim points a finger at his own head – 'is what's in here. It's not what some professor says it is. It's not even what's happening out there on the streets. It's what I make of it all in here,' he adds, tapping his forehead with a bony index finger.

'Isn't that making it all very subjective?'

'Exactly. What matters is what I see through the prism of my own sensibility.'

'You're close to solipsism now, aren't you?'

'Am I?'

'I think so.'

Finkleheim frowns. 'Then let's have some drinks.

Ireland is beckoning.'

Meryl rolls her eyes. 'That's where history is demonic, for chrissakes!'

'Which is precisely why we need drink.'

46

The Lubbocks' Diaries – Extract Seven:

The labyrinthine coils of the Celtic imagination! Finkleheim isn't a Celt; he's a Brahmin from Newark. But he's so caught up in the whole Irish thing he's beginning to think like a Celt. He wants to desacralize history, on the one hand, and here he is on the other hand, rushing to Ireland with an outdated manifesto to try to make a little bit of history of his own. Mind you, the manifesto may be outdated, but the idea it espouses is by no means out of date. And in politics timing is everything. What's right this week can be very wrong next week in terms of its acceptability. And in a hyped-up situation, a situation of intense emotions like the Irish one, even an outdated document can take on exaggerated importance. If nothing else the Provos will want to get their hands on it to shout 'sell out' or 'betrayal' or 'treachery'. And others besides the Provos. History has a way of trapping all of us.

47

They find Senator Michael D. Higgins in the Visitor's Bar of Leinster House reading the latest issue of *Hot Press* and eating a peanut butter sandwich. On his coat there is a big 'Save Nicaragua' badge. The chairman of the Labour Party is in fine form and greets them with a smile. 'Nice to see you again,' he tells Gene.

Finkleheim grasps his hand and introduces Sheri MacFerson. Meryl is not with them. She has arranged to meet another politician in a pub off O'Connell Street in the centre of Dublin. The lobbying has begun. 'This press conference has got to be a knock out,' she tells Gene before they part after the journey from Shannon.

'I can't really say much just now,' Gene tells Michael D. 'But we've got something really hot and we'd like you to be there to hear for yourself.'

'I'll be pleased to be there,' replies the Labour Party chairman. Other TDs and Senators crowd into the bar and there is a brief lull in the conversation when Avril Doyle drifts past in leather trousers.

Gene grasps Sheri by the hand and elbows his way through the legislators and the hangers-on. One thought is worrying him. Can they name names? Will it be prudent? More important, will it be fair and just? He verbalises the thought in the bar of Buswell's Hotel across the road from Leinster House.

'Do you mean – am I sure Jack Lynch knew about the Kennedy document?'

'Yeah. It's bothering me a bit.'

'Why?'

Finkleheim grimaces. 'It's something I'd like to be absolutely sure about, that's all . . . .'

'I don't have documentary proof, if that's what you mean. I've already told Meryl McClone that.'

'I appreciate that.'

'Look, we don't have to lay this at Lynch's doorstep if you don't want to. Maybe he didn't know. I don't think it matters all that much. We don't have to lay it on anyone at this end. It's enough that the offer was broached from the Washington end.'

'I guess you're right.'

A girl comes and places drinks on the table. They look uncertainly at each other. Sheri can see the concern in Gene's eyes. 'You know, I always took the view that a hard-headed pragmatic Taoiseach at this end would go for a NATO deal with Washington in exchange for an economic aid package,' she tells him, reiterating what she had said earlier to Meryl at their meeting in Battery Park. 'What's the big hang-up anyway? Ireland's neutrality isn't going to count one little bit. So why posture about it? For what – for moral self-righteousness? Do a deal with Washington and push a hard bargain – that's what I'd do.'

Finkleheim tries to fit Lynch into the context the girl has just sketched out and remains sceptical. 'That might work now or in the near future. I'm not sure it would have worked then or at any time in between, though I can't help thinking that when Lynch got that massive 20-seat majority in 1977 he could have sold anything to the country if the political will had been there – NATO bases, nuclear power stations, or even condom slot machines at every street corner. He could have steamrolled any kind of legislation through the Dáil.'

'You missed your calling.'

'What does that mean?'

'You should have been a politician.'

'One would still have to do battle with history, especially if one were a politician in Ireland. History is like a web here, an all-enveloping web which places constraints on everybody.'

'And freedom – what about that?' inquires Sheri, thoughtfully.

'Sometimes I think the Irish are afraid of freedom.

They haven't yet grasped it with both hands. They still live in a culture of dependence where it is cosy to shift the responsibility onto others, either dead or alive.'

'Freedom is the antidote to history.'

'I agree. The lesson for this generation of Irish men and women is clear. They have the right to choose what they want to become and without reference to 1916, 1921, 1966 or 1969. They are not obliged to regard the 1916 Proclamation as a sacred text or to regard what the seven signatories did or said as being in any way normative for them and their time. Those men felt free to make certain decisions and to embark on a certain course of action. They did that in good faith, and this generation doesn't have to sit in judgment on them. Neither, however, does this generation have to view themselves as recipients of an incomplete heritage or as ones to whom some sort of unfinished task has been entrusted. They don't have to subscribe to the cause or the aims of the men of 1916, nor do they have to feel constrained by their methods or entrapped by their deaths . . . .'

'But they do . . . .'

'I know, and that's one of the awful effects of history. This generation, those people out there on the streets of Dublin and across in Leinster House have and must claim the same right and the same freedom to make their own decisions for this time and the circumstances of the present, for now. And to the extent that they fail to do this then they possess an inadequate understanding of both freedom and history.'

'Is that why you're here?'

Finkleheim reflects for a moment. 'In part, I guess. This is what our project is about, mine and Meryl's and now you are part of it too. This is one of the key

113

lessons of the Lynch years, and why getting a perspective on Lynch and on those years is so important. And they're not over, they didn't end with the resignation of Jack Lynch. In a sense, the next ten or twenty years in Ireland will still be "The Lynch Years" because the struggle between freedom and history – which is the main characteristic of the period – and we're talking about yesterday, today and tomorrow, has only intensified. It is not over, not by any means . . . .'

48

Two women hold Meryl McClone by the arms.

A third, a skinny woman, a girl really for she is only nineteen, with a shock of pink hair cut punk-style and a black eyepatch, starts to strip her.

Meryl wants to scream but can't: they have tied a handkerchief over her mouth.

They are in an upstairs room of a disused house just off Mountjoy Square. The two men in the Balaclava headgear who took Meryl at gunpoint from the pub near O'Connell Street, are standing guard outside the room.

Inside the stripping of Meryl is almost complete. Only her bra and panties remain, and the pink-haired one-eyed girl uses a scissors to remove these.

One of the women holding Meryl giggles. 'Just look at those boobs,' she mutters.

'That's enough of that,' the girl with the eyepatch tells her sternly. 'Take her over to the bed . . . .'

They drag Meryl to the bed which is also stripped. All the clothes are gone and so is the mattress. It is an old bed with an all-metal frame and a metal springboard. This creaks furiously when Meryl is laid out on it, face upwards. Working quickly, the three women spreadeagle her and fasten her hands and feet to the four metal bedposts, using pieces of blue nylon rope. They stand back and Meryl begins to writhe and twist but she has only very limited movement.

'Will I take the gag off?' one of the women asks.

The girl with the eyepatch takes a pack of cigarettes from her pocket and shakes her head. 'Not yet. Let's give the bitch a taste of what's to come if she doesn't talk . . . .'

The third woman walks to the corner of the room to a box with a switch on it. One end of the box is linked by a black cable to a wall socket, the other end by two wires and electrode clips to both sides of the bedframe.

The woman by the box looks at the one-eyed one. The latter gestures. 'Turn it on, but not too much. We don't want to fry the bitch – not just yet anyway.'

As the electrical power surges through the wires and the metal bedframe Meryl bucks and arches her back as the shocks hit her.

The one-eyed one moves closer. 'All of this can end if you tell us where the Kennedy document is. But take your time. We're in no hurry . . . .'

She starts to laugh and gestures to the woman by the box to turn up the power. She laughs as well.

49

Steve McQueen has his hand on Ludmilla Erebus's left breast when the call from Doctor Lubbocks comes over the intercom. McQueen listens to the message, his hand still in place over Ludmilla's erect nipple.

'Fuck it, I have to go,' he tells her.

'I thought you came here to fuck me?'

'Later, honey, later. First I gotta go sort out some punks.'

McQueen removes his hand and bends to kiss Ludmilla's breast. 'I'll see you later.'

'Don't take too long.'

'Trust me,' he says, heading for the transporter room.

* * *

At the corner of Mountjoy Square McQueen pays off the taxi. He's carrying a long canvas bag, the kind used by hockey players. At the house where Meryl McClone is being held he notices scaffolding in front. Great. He slings the canvas bag over his shoulder and begins to climb. According to Doctor Lubbocks the girl is being held in a back room on the third storey. When he reaches that level McQueen peers through a dirty window and sees an empty room. He works on the window, opens it, climbs inside and unzips the canvas bag. From it he extracts a pump-action shotgun and a box of cartridges. He loads the weapon and moves cautiously out into the corridor to search for Meryl.

To his left the corridor stretches away until it runs into a blank wall; to his right it turns a corner. Faint sounds can be heard from that direction.

McQueen moves towards them, pauses at the corner, glances around very carefully and sees two men in trenchcoats standing outside a room door.

He pushes himself into view, the shotgun cocked and ready.

'Freeze!' he shouts.

The men turn, alarm showing in their faces. And then they make a mistake. They reach for their guns.

Too late.

McQueen fires and the massive blast from the shotgun catches the nearest man in the chest and hurls him along the corridor.

McQueen, grim-faced, works the pump action and fires again.

The second man goes down in a bloody heap, his trenchcoat torn apart.

'Shit, they should've got Clint Eastwood for this,' McQueen says, talking out loud to the dead men and looking just like he did in that hotel shoot-out in El Paso in Sam Peckinpah's 'Getaway'.

'I'm getting too old for stuff like this,' he says, still talking, as he forces open the door.

He spots Meryl McClone, still naked and still spreadeagled on the bed.

'The cavalry has arrived,' he calls out as he approaches to free her. 'I'd close my eyes, but it wouldn't do any good.'

'Oh God, I'm so scared,' she tells him, sitting up, rubbing her wrists and shaking with cold and fear and fright.

'You can relax, honey. It's all over. Those punks ain't gonna bother you no more.' McQueen grins. He's finding it hard to stop looking at Ms McClone's tits. You would too, believe me.

'Where are your things?'

'Over there,' replies Meryl, getting off the bed and walking stiffly to the corner where her clothes have been thrown. Across her shoulders, her backside and the rear of her legs there are red marks. 'I have to get to a telephone,' she tells him as she puts on a blouse. 'I told them where the document is. I had to.'

McQueen is studying the box with the wires; he

doesn't have to be told what happened. With the butt of the shotgun he smashes it. 'Who did you tell – the guys outside?'

'No. There were three others. Three women. They left to pick up the document. It's too late to stop them now, but I have to warn the others . . . .'

'Gee, I'm real sorry about that, honey. I got here as soon as I could.'

Meryl's composure is returning. She is almost fully dressed. 'That doesn't matter now. What matters is that the others should be told. We must warn them.'

'I'm ready whenever you are.'

'Is there a 'phone close by?'

'There's a kiosk on the street corner,' McQueen informs her, jerking a thumb.

'Okay. Let's get out of here.'

'I'm with you, honey . . . .'

50

Eamonn McCann has joined Finkleheim and Sheri MacFerson in the bar of Buswell's. Gene wants him in on the press conference. McCann orders a glass of Perrier. Ms MacFerson resumes where she left off when the man from *The Sunday World* came in.

'Lynch has consistently said that the tactics of the Provisional IRA today "would have been anathema to the Old IRA whom they spuriously claim to succeed", and that's a direct quote. Gerry Adams, on the other hand, claims the mantle of the Old IRA for the Provos. And he accuses constitutional nationalists like Mr Lynch who pay homage each year to Old IRA men – while condemning the Provisional IRA – of indulging in verbal and intellectual gymnastics. Isn't there a breakdown in logic somewhere here . . . .?'

Finkleheim looks to McCann. 'What do you think, Eamonn?'

'There are no ifs, buts or maybes in the matter of who is right and who is wrong in this argument,' replies McCann in his staccato Derry accent. 'Gerry Adams is right. Jack Lynch is wrong. This doesn't mean that the Provisional IRA is, in a moral sense, "right". What it means is that the Provos are in the tradition of Sean Tracey, for instance, and Jack Lynch is not, even though both Adams and Lynch have spoken at the annual Sean Tracey commemoration at Kilfeakle in County Tipperary. Adams is right when he says the Provos are in the tradition of Sean Tracey and Jack Lynch is not. What you make of that depends on what you make of Sean Tracey . . . .'

'Do you know about Sean Tracey?' Finkleheim asks Ms MacFerson.

'Yes. He was involved with Dan Breen in the Soloheadbeg Ambush of January, 1919.'

McCann continues: 'It is possible consistently and logically to reject what Sean Tracey and Gerry Adams represent, or to support what they both represent. But it is not possible consistently and honestly to condone the one and to condemn the other. And it is surely about time that constitutional nationalism in Ireland acquired the maturity to face the implications of this fact.'

'Another case of historical double-think, would you say?' asks Ms MacFerson.

'I guess so,' replies Finkleheim.

Just then he hears himself being paged over the hotel's PA system.

At the reception desk he is told there is a telephone call for him.

It is Meryl.

She tells him about her abduction, and her disclosure under torture of the whereabouts of *The Kennedy Manifesto*.

'Jesus Christ,' he intones, the colour draining from his face.

51

The *'Zintanza'* has landed in the Phoenix Park not far from where Pope John Paul II said Mass during his historic Irish visit. On board Doctor Lubbocks is preoccupied. He is watching the screen in front of him.

In between the rusting hulks of old cars and battered oil drums, a man sits and waits. He is wearing a stetson. It has a name stitched on the sweatband. Doctor Lubbocks adjusts the controls to get a close-up of the name.

'Haughey.'

The man sits there – waiting. He is holding a gun in his hand.

The sun is sinking in the West.

And the buzzards are overhead.

The man breaks open the Colt .45, checks the chambers, spins the cylinder, and snaps it shut.

And he waits. And waits.

Doctor Lubbocks, puzzled, watches intently. The screen he is looking at is linked to equipment on board the spaceship with the capability for seeing into the future. The good Doctor is flummoxed.

Ludmilla Erebus enters. The Doctor looks around. 'We've got a problem,' she announces.

'What is it?' he asks, absent-mindedly.

'The girl is okay. Steve McQueen rescued her. But she has lost the document.'

The Doctor presses another button on the console and another screen flickers into life. He watches Steve McQueen and Meryl McClone walking away from a telephone box.

'I monitored the call,' Ludmilla tells him.

'What a pity,' muses the Doctor. 'It could have been very interesting. Now I shall have to intervene personally.'

He reaches across and pushes a blue switch. 'There, that takes care of the document.' He turns to Ms Erebus and smiles: he hasn't done that all day. 'Mr McQueen will be back shortly, and you shall have your reward.'

'Oh good,' exclaims Ludmilla, embracing the Doctor.

'Control yourself, woman,' he tells her gruffly, freeing himself from her arms.

She giggles to herself as he leaves the control room of the spacecraft.

52

Across Dublin in a terraced house in Malahide a bearded young man wearing glasses and a tweed jacket puffs on his pipe and permits a thin anticipatory smile to drift across his face as he opens the document in front of him. On the cover in stark black letters are the words: 'The Kennedy Manifesto'.

On the other side of the table three women wait in silence, their nervousness almost palpable. One of them has pink hair and a black eyepatch.

The bearded man turns the first couple of pages and his expression changes. The smile has vanished.

He turns more pages. And some more. He looks up sharply at the three women.

'What is going on here?' he barks.

The trio exchange nervous, uncertain glances. No word passes from their lips.

'All these pages are blank. There is nothing here. We've been tricked!'

The women are now displaying signs of distress. They know how much Gerry Adams, President of Provisional Sinn Féin, dislikes being tricked.

He glowers across at them, flings the useless document to the floor and storms out.

There are no giggles at this exit.

53

'Who is this?'

The query comes from Gene Finkleheim. He is in 'The Horse and Tram' on Eden Quay having left McCann at Buswell's after receiving the telephone message. He has decided that going to a halfway location with Sheri MacFerson to meet Meryl McClone will help his nerves. On the way he fills Sheri in on what has transpired.

Meryl has just come into the bar with a strange man.

'This is Doctor Ernst Lubbocks,' she tells Gene.

'Who is he?' he asks, without much graciousness.

Before Meryl can answer Doctor Lubbocks intervenes. 'I am a friend.'

'Where did you pick him up?' asks Gene

impatiently, ignoring the stranger.

'He said he has come from the Phoenix Park.'

'So now what do we do with him?' Gene wants to know, the sarcasm showing. The loss of the document has taken him close to his wit's end. And now this unwanted intrusion.

'Why don't we just buy him a pint,' suggests Meryl equably, 'and listen to what he has to say . . . .?'

Capitulating, Gene summons the barman. 'Maybe, we could all do with a drink.'

'You need worry no longer about the document,' the Doctor assures him, having read his thoughts.

'How can you say that?' shouts Gene.

Doctor Lubbocks smiles tolerantly.

'He has a spaceship,' Meryl informs Gene.

'What?'

'A spaceship,' repeats Meryl. 'It's hidden in the Phoenix Park.'

Gene looks hard at the man; something about him is familiar. He's sure of that much. 'Who are you? Or what are you?'

'I am a time-traveller,' the Doctor replies. 'A friendly one.'

Finkleheim grinds his teeth and scratches his beard. 'What can you do for us?'

'I can make it possible for you to try again.'

'To do what?'

'To make – or remake – history.'

'Just like that?'

'Well, the context will have to be different. And the time.'

'We blew it,' snarls Finkleheim, partly in self-annoyance.

'The intention was good. That's why I'm here. Do you want to try again?'

The drinks arrive. Finkleheim distributes them. He

stares hard at Doctor Lubbocks, and then turns to Meryl and Sheri. 'Well, girls, what do you think? We're all in this together.'

The girls exchange looks. Sheri nods to Meryl almost imperceptibly.

'We've come this far,' says Meryl. 'Why should we quit now?'

Finkleheim shrugs and smiles.

'So you'll come with me?' inquires Doctor Lubbocks.

'Where to?' Finkleheim wants to know.

'To another galaxy perhaps. For a while anyway.'

Gene looks again at Meryl. 'What do you think?'

'I thought it was decided.'

'Ah fuck it, why not? I'm tired of this place anyway and its festival of destruction. We all need a break . . . .'

'Okay folks, drink up,' Doctor Lubbocks tells them. 'The future is beckoning.'

54

The Lubbocks' Diaries – Extract Eight:
There is a time and a place for mysticism. And magic. And this could be it.

55

Drinks are served by the delectable duo, Ms Bachinski and Ms Erebus. The *'Zintanza'* is over the Canary Islands when Doctor Lubbocks switches on the large video screen in the spaceship's main leisure theatre.

The words 'An Easter Prizing' appear and are replaced by a succession of images – Seagull-Connolly; Finkleheim-Pearse; Lubbocks-McDonagh; Bachinski-Plunkett; McClone-Countess; Lynch-Cowboy; Haughey-Cowboy; Adams-FBI Man; Castro-FBI Man; Leone-Punk IRA Girl; McQueen-McCann.

Suddenly all the figures merge and coalesce until only the figure of a statuesque blonde remains.

She is wearing a long dark-green coat and high suede boots of matching colour. Her expression is solemn as she declares: 'My name is Kathleen Houlihan – no relation of Con's . . . .'

Her lovely turquoise eyes begin to twinkle. The solemn expression gives way to a wicked grin as she flings open the coat and FLASHES her naked and superb body.

Her teasing mocking laughter is everywhere.

ZOOM SHOT: The image that finally fills the screen is a forest of Kathleen Houlihan's pubic hairs. From amongst these a tiny figure is visible.

The face of the figure – it is a man – looks remarkably like Jack Lynch's.

As the manic laughter trails off one word is audible: 'HELP!'

FADE OUT